⍋ **W9-BDJ-327**

The Dare to Love Series and NY Dares Series

Dare to Love Series
Book 1: *Dare to Love* (Ian & Riley)
Book 2: *Dare to Desire* (Alex & Madison)
Book 3: *Dare to Touch* (Olivia & Dylan)
Book 4: *Dare to Hold* (Scott & Meg)
Book 5: *Dare to Rock* (Avery & Grey)
Book 6: *Dare to Take* (Tyler & Ella)

NY Dares Series
Book 1: *Dare to Surrender* (Gabe & Isabelle)
Book 2: *Dare to Submit* (Decklan & Amanda)
Book 3: *Dare to Seduce* (Max & Lucy)

The NY Dares books are more erotic/hotter books.

Dear Reader,

The NY Dares are the cousins of the Dare to Love series characters. These three books, *Dare to Surrender, Dare to Submit,* and *Dare to Seduce,* all contain exceptionally hotter content—including erotic BDSM elements—while still being emotional Carly Phillips stories.

Thank you for joining me for the ride, and enjoy!

All the best,
Carly

CONTENTS

Chapter One

*M*ax Savage glanced across the lush green lawn of Gabriel and Isabelle Dare's Bedford, New York, home, his gaze focused on the sexy brunette he couldn't get out of his head. Lucy Dare, dressed in a conservative pantsuit, her luxurious dark hair pulled into a bun, stood beside her date, a Hollywood director who was a douchebag of the first order.

The last time Max had seen Lucy, she'd been her wild and free self. Then she'd hooked up with that guy, and she'd changed. And not in a good way. He wanted fun, sexy Lucy back.

"How badly do you want to punch that guy's teeth in?"

"So badly," Max muttered, then glanced over, realizing the question came from Lucy's brother, Decklan Dare.

Max shook his head and changed his answer, because it would do no good to let his best friend know he was obsessing over the guy's little sister. He'd kept it to himself for years, partially as an excuse to deny what he really wanted, but regardless, this wasn't the right time to bring up the issue.

"Who do you mean?" Max asked.

Decklan rolled his eyes. "Oh, come on. I know you hate that Spielberg wannabe as much as we do."

"Can't say he'd be my first choice for your sister."

"That's rich, considering it's your fault she's with him to begin with." Decklan eyed Max with distinct annoyance in his gaze.

"How the hell do you figure *that*?" Max asked.

Decklan's older brother, Gabe, joined them, and from the look on his face, he'd clearly caught the tail end of the conversation.

"Face it, Savage. We know you have a thing for Lucy," Gabe said.

Just how the brothers had gleaned that bit of knowledge was beyond Max. Nobody had a better poker face than him.

Decklan merely nodded in agreement.

"You didn't take your chance last time she was in town, and now she's with that asshole," Gabe added, angling his head toward where his sister stood with Lucas Kellan.

"Well, fuck." Max wasn't about to deny what had clearly been more obvious than he'd intended.

Both Dare brothers narrowed their gazes on him, waiting for an explanation.

"What? I didn't think you'd approve, and I wasn't about to mess up years' worth of friendship if you didn't." He was sticking to the tried-and-true excuse he'd told himself for years. In reality, Max had his reasons for staying away from Lucy for so long and for fucking up more than just his life in the process. But they were his, and he wouldn't be sharing them.

"The only way you'd compromise friendships would be if you used or hurt my sister. If your intentions are honorable, I have no issue," said Gabe, the man who'd raised Lucy after their parents died in a car accident.

Max glanced at Decklan. They both knew Max's recent past. He'd married young, lost his wife, Cindy, in a car accident, and had a subsequent lack of serious relationships since. What Decklan didn't know was the guilt Max harbored over the emotions he hadn't been able to give his wife, due to the feelings he'd always had for Lucy. Hell, he'd married Cindy because he didn't have those intense feelings, and everyone had paid a price.

Max shifted uncomfortably and cleared his throat and glanced at Decklan, who, like Gabe, was extremely protective of his sister. "You too? You're okay with this?" he asked.

His best friend shrugged. "Well, you're an asshole, but you're our asshole." He slapped Max on the back, his expression sobering. "Look, Cindy died four years ago, and you haven't been with anyone seriously since."

Neither one of them mentioned Max's penchant for sex clubs on the weekends. It had been a way to fill the emptiness inside him, nothing more.

"But Gabe is right," Decklan said. "I see how you look at Lucy. You should do something about it if your intentions are solid."

They finally were. For years, Max had denied his need for Lucy and the emotional bond he knew they would share if they took things to the next level. Fear had driven him. Now Max was finally ready to go after the woman he'd always wanted.

"Just don't blow it, or we will have an issue," Decklan cheerfully added.

Max didn't need to be told twice. He made his way across the lawn and veered between guests, coming up to where Lucy and her date stood by the bar. Before he could interrupt, he caught their conversation.

"I hope we don't need to stay much longer." Lucas glanced at the ostentatious gold watch on his wrist, his impatience obvious. "I have calls to make, so I'd like to get back to the hotel soon."

Lucy's eyes opened wide. "It's my brother's engagement party! I'm staying until the end. Longer, even, so I can spend time with my family."

Lucas ran a hand over the top of his stylishly cut blond hair. Looked like Lucy had a type, too. Not that Max thought he had anything more in common with the director than hair color.

"Come on, babe. You live in LA, and your brothers are way across the country here in New York, so how much do you really want to spend time with them? We've been here an hour. I say we're good to go," Lucas said, cementing Max's gut feeling. The man was an uncaring ass.

What kind of asshole got between a woman and her family? Max wondered, curling his hands into tight fists. And how could Lucy be with the bastard if he didn't understand what her brothers meant to her and why?

Her pretty eyes filled with angry, frustrated tears. "You leave then. I want to be here."

Lucas studied her face for a beat, clearly assessing whether she was serious. "Fine, we'll stay." He didn't sound gracious about the concession. "But I'm going to need to make a few calls from the car. Okay?" Before she could answer, he nodded. "Okay." He had the gall to wink at her, then leaned over and placed a quick peck on her lips.

Max's fists grew tighter. Part of him was disgusted by the other man's mouth on hers; another knew a woman like Lucy deserved more than that pathetic excuse for a kiss. If she belonged to him, he'd seal his lips over hers and thoroughly devour her luscious mouth. He'd make sure his tongue swiped through the deep recesses of her mouth so his taste lingered inside her long after they parted. And he'd damn well ensure that he left her lips puffy and well kissed, so no other man would try to make a move on his female.

Caveman mentality? Maybe. But those were the feelings Lucy Dare stirred inside him.

Instead of waiting until lover boy walked away, Max strode over and slid an arm around her waist. "Hey, princess." He'd been calling her that since she'd turned sixteen and spent the day wearing a crown. As she'd grown up, the nickname had stuck.

"Max! I didn't see you arrive," she said, startled.

"Business meeting. I ran late," he explained.

"And I want to hear all about the newest restaurant you're planning and which chef you've managed to lure away from which pissed-off restaurateur."

Max grinned, excited to share the details with her. Very few knew about his plans. He was waiting to do a press release and promo op with his choice.

"You know me well." Since her boyfriend was busy glancing at his phone, Max cleared his throat and said, "Aren't you going to introduce us?"

Lucy blushed. "Max Savage, this is—"

"Lucas Kellan," the other man said, shaking Max's hand in a limp grip. "I'm a director out in Hollywood."

"Oh? I thought you were Lucy's boyfriend. Seems to me that's what's important here."

"Max," Lucy chided, clearly not wanting him to cause trouble.

Lucas frowned at Max. "I'm both. I just thought you might have seen my movies—"

Max turned to Lucy. "We need to talk."

"But—" She glanced at her boyfriend.

"Go on," Lucas said. "He'll keep you busy while I'm working. Hell, he can take my place with your family for a little while." He dismissed Max, and his focus returned to his cell phone.

Either he wasn't smart enough to realize Max was a threat, or he just didn't care, because he strode off, heading for the yard exit.

"What the hell are you doing with a dickhead like that?" Max couldn't help but ask her.

Lucy spun around to face him, her cheeks flushed with embarrassment. "He's in the middle of a big deal that's stressful and—"

"Don't make excuses for him."

She folded her arms across her chest, and though she showed no cleavage, the movement pulled the silk material across her full breasts, revealing tight, perky nipples. Max's cock shot to attention, and he shifted his stance to alleviate the sudden discomfort.

She caught his gaze and frowned. "Quit staring at my breasts, you pervert." She followed that statement with a roll of her eyes.

He shook his head at her reaction. If he were at Paradis, the BDSM club he attended in Manhattan, he'd pull her over his knee and give her a good spanking. Another reason he'd stayed away from Lucy recently. In the years since his marriage, he'd discovered his tastes weren't always purely vanilla. But as he'd watched Lucy mature, he'd sensed she'd suit him fine. Outside the bedroom, she gave him hell, but his gut told him that once he showed her how good they could be together, she'd submit nicely in the bedroom. Hell, if he had Lucy, he wouldn't care about domination or submission. Those things had let him control something when the rest of his life felt out of control. All he really needed with Lucy was good, hot sex.

He reached out and placed his hand beneath her chin, tipping her face until she met his gaze. "Admit it. You like the way I'm looking at you."

She blinked in stunned surprise because he was changing the game. They'd always sparred . . . and steered clear of the underlying sexual tension that surrounded them, which often led to arguing over nothing. Not this time. He intended to confront that sexual tension head on.

"Come with me." He grasped her wrist and tugged.

She resisted, then finally gave in, following him across the lawn and around the corner of the colonial-style house, where they could be alone. He stopped at a large cypress tree that probably predated construction and pulled her behind the trunk.

"Max, I don't think this is a good idea."

He spun her around until her back was against the trunk and stepped in close. Her delicious scent surrounded him, a mixture of peaches and something else. His gut twisted while his cock swelled even more.

For the first time, he wasn't fighting what he felt for her, what he needed.

"I think this is the very best idea."

Her cheeks flushed a healthy pink, her eyes bright with confusion. "I don't understand."

He reached up and sunk his hands into her hair, dislodging the staid updo she wouldn't be wearing if not for her asshole boyfriend, and tugged his fingers through the long strands.

"Max!"

She reached up to fix herself, but he caught her wrists in his hands and backed her farther into the tree, his body firmly nestled against her softness. His erection settled between her thighs, hot and hard, begging for relief and release. No way could she miss how much he wanted her.

She met his gaze, her eyes wide with surprise and darkening with desire.

"Answer my question, Lucy. What are you doing with that guy?"

"Oh my God. Lucas!" she said. Obviously she'd forgotten all about the man, and now she shifted in an attempt to get free.

Max held her firmly in place.

"I shouldn't be here with you," she said, but the heat in her eyes didn't match her words.

"You should definitely be here with me. So you can feel us, then take a good look at that so-called relationship you're in and do something about it."

Lucy heard his words and tried to fight her body's opposing response. Panicking, she tried once more to wriggle out of his grasp, but Max's strong, hard body held her in place.

His sandalwood scent enveloped her and softened places in her body she barely acknowledged these days. Her nipples were tight and hard, poking through her silk blouse, and her sex pulsed with unaccustomed need. This was *Max*. And yes, she'd had a crush on him for years, but that was a long time ago, and she'd been forced to accept that he didn't see her *that* way.

Hell, he'd married someone else when she was twenty-three and so available that she'd have done anything to make him her own. His engagement had been a blow, one that had hit her already-bruised heart harder than she ever could have imagined. She'd lost her parents and built stupid forever dreams around Max Savage. He may not have known, but when he'd married someone else, Lucy had been devastated.

She'd grasped on to another dream, being in charge of decor for the family clubs, and headed to California. Not only hadn't she come home for Max's wedding, but, on see-ing the invitation, she'd decided to remain in LA for good. She'd suffered enough loss and pain to last a lifetime. With her brothers moving forward, finding good women to love, Lucy knew she wasn't needed here.

Losing Max—though she'd never really had him—had forced her to toughen up. She chose men she didn't have a chance of falling head over heels in love with, men whose loss wouldn't gut her. She had forced herself to return home for Max's wife's funeral, understanding all too well what grief and loss were like.

That was four long years ago. They'd since returned to their sibling-like bickering whenever they were together. Her last trip home, she'd actually wondered if the arguing was a way to cover sexual tension, but she'd pushed the idea deep down and far away, telling herself she was crazy. He'd never really given any indication he thought of her *that* way.

Until now.

When his chiseled, muscled body held her prisoner against the tree and her body thrummed with such intense need, she was seconds away from wriggling her hips and mov-ing shamelessly against him. From grinding herself into his thick, hard erection and taking what she needed until she came—screaming—and the party guests surrounded them to find out what the ruckus was about.

She couldn't cross that line with Max. They shared a complicated relationship as it was, with a depth of emotion and caring she'd never felt for another man. And that made him dangerous to her mental and emotional well-being.

She gathered her strength and met his gaze. "What's going on, Max? You see me with another man, and you decide to get jealous all of a sudden?"

His dirty-blond hair fell over his forehead, and she curled her hands into fists, resisting the urge to brush it back. Heck, it wasn't just his hair she was dying to touch.

"Am I jealous?" He shrugged. "Only that you're here with him. I'm not particularly worried you're going to stay with him though."

The cords of his neck protruded, tight and tense, and she wasn't buying the attempt at nonchalance. "That's a cocky statement."

He let out a low, rumbling laugh she felt everywhere. "He doesn't appreciate you for who you are, princess."

"How would you know that?" she asked indignantly. Though a part of her knew he was right, Max was in no position to judge her or her choice in men.

"Let's begin with this." He slid a finger down her silk shirt, causing her already tight nipples to make their presence known even more. "While the soft material suits you fine, you like your clothes brighter, tighter, and showing more of that beautiful body."

He undid her blouse, button by tiny button, until she could breathe more freely and her cleavage was exposed. Her breath hitched, and she couldn't summon an argument, merely watched his big hands so close to her skin.

"You prefer a big piece of statement jewelry around your neck or letting that sexy tanned skin show. Mr. Uptight probably has his own requirements, though damned if I understand why he'd want to hide your light," he said as his roughened fingertips glided over her skin.

Her knees buckled, but Max's body weight supported her.

Still, she held on to rational thought. "Don't judge Lucas. He needs to project a certain image when he's approaching people to give money to his films."

"Then let him find a woman just like him. Not someone he needs to change. I wouldn't ask you to change for me." He cupped her neck in his hands, and a soft, needy moan escaped her lips.

"Max," she whispered.

"What?"

Don't do this. The words stuck in her throat because her body and a traitorous emotionally needy part of her wanted it. Wanted his mouth devouring hers, his talented hands gliding over her breasts, her nipples, and inside her sex. She desired him and had for years.

"Why now?" she asked in a feeble attempt to halt the inevitable.

"Because it's long past time." He brushed his thumb over her damp lips before covering her mouth with his.

She met him with a moan of acceptance. His lips were firm, moving with determination and a grace she wouldn't have expected, and his tongue glided back and forth, urging her to open and let him inside. One more swipe and she parted for him. He swept in, starting slow, learning his way, growing ever bolder.

Every lick, taste, and touch resonated inside her, her body alive and tingling in ways she'd never experienced before. His hands slid behind her neck, and his fingers thrust into her hair again. Her hair fell down her back, and he groaned, threaded his hands through, and tugged the strands, causing a sudden, delicious throbbing between her legs. A needy moan escaped from the back of her throat.

"You like that?" he asked, pulling harder on her hair.

She rocked her hips into his, the equivalent of a nod or a yes.

"Fuck." He tilted her head for better, deeper access and kissed her long and hard, a low groan of appreciation rumbling from deep in his chest.

He conquered her mouth, and she allowed him to take what he wanted, mutual desire flaring between them, the kiss now out of control. She'd given up the fight the minute his mouth had touched hers, and now she slid her hands through his silky hair and held on as he devoured her. Teeth clashed, tongues twined, and her breasts rubbed against his shirt, her aching nipples seeking what little relief she could find.

Every fantasy Lucy had had over the years didn't hold up to reality. This was so much better. No man had ever kissed her this way, as if he couldn't live without her taste, without *her*.

She was so lost in his taste and desire that she wasn't prepared when he broke the kiss, and she gasped for air. Somehow she'd been breathing through him, with him. He still held her up, more gently than before, his torso supporting her weight, his arms braced on either side of her head.

His eyes gleamed bright with desire and, if she wasn't mistaken, more than a hint of satisfaction . . . and that made her nervous.

"Now tell me, has anyone else made you feel like this?" he asked.

His words brought her back to reality, and horror set in. She'd succumbed to Max so easily, as if Lucas meant nothing to her at all. Which wasn't true.

She and Lucas had a comfortable relationship. He was someone to talk to, to have dinner with, and occasionally, when they were in the mood, sex was actually good. That was all she wanted. After all, if she didn't become emotionally invested, she couldn't be devastated when the relationship ended. And they all ended eventually.

"Is that what this was about, Max? Proving a point? That we have chemistry? Bravo. You proved you could seduce me if you wanted to." She braced her hands on his shoulders and shoved him away.

"This wasn't about some damned point. This was to show you what we could have. You weren't about to listen to words. I had to act."

"Well, you put me in an awful situation."

"I just want you to *think*. If you're honest, there's only one conclusion you can come to—give us a real chance."

She stared at him as if he'd lost his mind. Maybe she'd lost her hearing. "Are you crazy? Where were you years ago?" she asked, horror setting in when she realized what she'd admitted to.

Shaking, she turned away and ran for the house, adjusting her pantsuit as she made her way there. She was a mess, her hair tangled around her face, her lips swollen and clothes undone. She'd have to sneak inside if she really wanted to fix herself and hide the evidence of her betrayal. Isabelle wouldn't mind if Lucy used her things, so she'd head to the master bedroom and lock herself inside. Hopefully nobody would see her if she went in through the front and avoided the partygoers in the back.

She slipped into the main entrance and darted for the stairs, then enclosed herself in the master bath. Alone, she sighed and gripped the marble countertop hard. Max Savage had just kissed her. Hell, he'd ravaged her in broad daylight, and she'd let him. And he'd been the one to break the kiss, not her.

Lucy had never considered herself a cheater, so what had she been thinking? She shook her head, knowing the answer. She hadn't been. There'd been a time when she would have been ready for Max. When she'd still held on to fantasies of older, sexy Max Savage turning those amber eyes on her and claiming her as his own. Then he'd fallen in love and gotten married, shattering any foolish dreams of Max protecting her from the harsh outside world of loss.

Instead, he'd handed her more.

So she'd grown up and found safety in independence and distance. She'd graduated college, moved to California, helped decorate the family clubs her brother Gabe ran. Living on the West Coast, she could keep up with, and care about, Gabe and Decklan from afar. Protect herself and her heart . . .

should something tragic happen to them like it had to her parents. Being isolated had also prepared her for the day when her brothers found their own families . . . and they had. She could love from a distance. It was safer.

Lucas was a safe choice. She knew her brothers didn't like him, but they didn't understand him either. He was busy and usually preoccupied with whatever film he was working on at any given time, which made him come off as abrupt and uncaring. But weren't her brothers busy too? Gabe ran a nightclub empire, and Decklan had been promoted to police detective . . . but their women took priority. For Lucy, it had taken a lot of pleading to get Lucas to come to New York with her for her brother's engagement, and he still hadn't committed to joining her in Eden for the wedding. Still, he was here now.

And he wouldn't approve of this messy version of herself. In Hollywood, appearances were important, and she told herself she didn't mind playing a role, dressing the way he preferred. Not the way her family was used to. As she smoothed her blouse with shaking hands, she realized how well Max knew what she liked, how he preferred the real Lucy Dare.

She bit down on her lower lip, reminding herself it didn't matter what Max liked. She and Lucas were compatible. And if she didn't see fireworks when Lucas kissed her, so what? They clicked. Neither gave the other a hard time if they had to work late or couldn't see each other for long stretches. Unlike her brothers, who barely let Amanda and Isabelle out of their sight whenever possible. And the way they looked at their women . . . Max had looked at her that way, she thought with a full-body shiver, right before his lips had descended on hers.

She trembled, her entire body still singing from that nearly public, sizzling-hot, tongue-tangling, soul-touching kiss. She still hadn't recovered from the emotional assault on her senses, nor had she begun to figure out how she felt about it. Well, she knew how her body felt—her blood ran hot, her skin still tingled, and the kiss kept replaying on an endless loop in her brain. She had to refrain from running her fingers over her still-sensitive lips.

In the course of ten short minutes, Max Savage had ripped away any shred of safety and sanity she'd possessed, leaving her raw and fragile. If she ever were to get involved with Max, she'd fall hard, and if she lost him, she didn't know if she'd find her way back from the pain.

Somehow she refreshed her makeup, a swipe of blush on her cheeks and gloss on her well-kissed lips. She worked on her hair next, but each pass of the brush led to instant recall of Max's fingers pulling at the long strands and the way her sex had pulsed in reaction. She didn't understand the tug of desire that action had evoked, but she knew she'd never experienced such intense longing before. Even now, her panties were still damp, her body aching and needy. In the end, she didn't put her hair back up, unable to replicate the updo she'd had before.

She made her way down the stairs and headed back outside, finding Lucas at their rental car, which he was using as his makeshift office. "Lucas."

He held up one finger, indicating she should wait, and continued his phone call.

She glanced into the bright blue sky. Her brother and Amanda had lucked out with the weather, she thought as Lucas droned on. Finally, he disconnected the call.

"Ready to leave?" he asked hopefully.

She shook her head and groaned. He really wasn't interested in her family, her life, or the things and people that mattered to her. But she wasn't ready to give up on him yet.

He sat in the back seat, car door open, facing outside into the sun, jotting down notes.

"Lucas? What are we doing?"

"Going back to the hotel, where I can work in comfort, I hope."

She bit the inside of her cheek. "I'm staying, Lucas. If you keep complaining about being here and sitting in the car doing work, I'd rather you just went back to LA." She folded her arms across her aching chest. "But if you care about me, you'll stay here and try to get to know my family." Her voice quivered along with her insides.

No matter what, she hadn't traveled out here planning to end her relationship. She hadn't even considered the reasons she should. But now they were flittering around the edges of her mind . . . and she blamed Max. Max, who still might mess up everything she had in LA. Because if Lucas chose to stay and try to make things work, she'd have to tell him about that kiss and face the consequences. If he didn't choose to stick around, well, he was stating he didn't care enough to bother. In which case, she had no reason to hurt him with the knowledge. If he even cared enough to *be* hurt.

She met his gaze and waited.

He narrowed his gaze. "I don't understand. I thought we complemented each other. No muss, no fuss, no hassle." He sounded genuinely confused about why she was suddenly questioning things.

Though she'd thought about their relationship in much the same stark terms, hearing him phrase things so blandly hurt. Didn't she want to mean more to someone than that? Damn Max for stirring up all these feelings and realizations.

"I thought that was enough for me, but coming here and seeing my family again, realizing how happy my brothers are . . . I'm not sure it is."

He glanced at her through his dark sunglasses. "Wait one minute. What happened to your hair?" he asked, narrowing his gaze as he obviously really looked at her for the first time.

She ran a hand down the long strands, no longer pinned back tight the way he preferred. "I—"

"And your blouse is unbuttoned." His jaw clenched. "You know I don't like you looking like . . . like a tramp."

She flinched. "Something happened . . . with Max." She swallowed hard and forced herself to continue despite the cruel sting of his words. "I was going to tell you. I didn't initiate it, but he kissed me. I'm sorry, but—"

Lucas rose and stood too close, anger vibrating off his body. "You didn't suddenly look at your brothers' relationships and decide that what we shared wasn't enough for you. Jesus Christ. You fucking kissed that guy, and now you're giving me an ultimatum you know damn well I won't accept."

"Lucas—"

She reached out for him, but he flung off her touch and attempt to calm him.

"It didn't mean anything," she assured him, even as her pounding heart and memories of Max's sexy mouth and hot body declared her words a lie. But she couldn't let inconvenient feelings mess up her well-ordered life. She wanted the safe and easy relationship she and Lucas shared.

"I took precious time off from work and traveled all the way out here, and you cheated on me like a common whore." He slammed the back door hard.

She jumped at the sound, shocked at his crude words. "It wasn't like that."

"Don't fucking talk to her like that." Max stepped between them while Lucy stood stunned. Lucas's words had hit too close to home, and he'd never spoken to her like that before.

Lucas glared at Max, clearly assessing his angry competition. Max boxed for sport and fitness. Lucas didn't. From the tight clench of Max's fists to the muscles bulging in his forearms, he was damned close to taking a swing.

"I don't have time for this bullshit or for you," Lucas finally muttered. He stalked past her, brushing his shoulder against hers as he headed for the driver's seat.

"Touch her again and you'll be picking your teeth up off the ground one by one," Max muttered.

"Screw you." Lucas closed himself inside the Lincoln Town Car, started the engine, floored the gas, and drove away without looking back.

Lucy closed her eyes, hating how things had turned out between them. She'd rather have ended things the right way, but Max had forced the issue.

And she hadn't pushed him away.

Chapter Two

*M*ax watched Lucy's ex drive away, a combination of satisfaction and wariness eating at his gut. He'd charged in where he wasn't invited and turned her life upside down. He felt bad. But he couldn't say he was sorry.

Years. He'd waited years for this woman, believing in his heart and soul he would never have her. He'd even married another in the vain hopes of putting Lucy out of his mind and destroyed Cindy in the process.

The night his wife had died, they'd had a fight, just one of many. She'd wanted more from him than he was capable of giving her. She'd wanted him home more, devoting his nights to her instead of to his business. She'd grabbed her keys and run out crying. The cops said she probably never saw the truck until it swerved into her lane. She was gone in an instant.

And he had to live with the knowledge that he'd never have been able to love her the way he should've. And she'd known it as well. It'd taken years of self-exploration, some of it through his friendships with people in the BDSM world, to really see himself and his issues . . . and put them behind him. He'd had to come to terms with the fact that he'd done to Cindy what his parents had done to him. Held out the promise of love, caring, and a wonderful life only to fail in the execution. He'd emulated what he'd known, and that had been a mistake.

It helped that one guy in particular was a shrink who had no problem giving advice outside the office to people he cared about. Those long talks with Daniel Carver, who was still a close friend, and the ensuing years of learning to forgive himself had helped get Max ready for Lucy. Unfortunately, she'd arrived with the asshole.

Max turned his focus to the present. To Lucy. "You're better off without him, you know. No guy should speak to you that way." Lucas Kellan had been fortunate to get away with his pretty face intact.

Lucy shook her head, her dark-blue eyes full of anger and frustration. "Go away, Max."

"Can't do that, princess."

She sighed. "Then do me the supreme favor of getting lost for a little while."

Now that the jerk was gone and there was nobody around but family and friends to worry about, Max could give her the space she needed. "I won't be far. And when you've calmed down, we will have a long talk about *us*."

She shot him a withering glare, and without a word, she stormed back toward the house.

He shoved his hands into his pants pockets and watched her go. Her long hair swung back and forth as she moved. The woman had a killer body, and her cream-colored pants suit accented her curves. He was an ass man, and Lucy's did it for him. It was round and perfect enough to fit in his hands, and he couldn't wait to grip her naked cheeks. But he was getting ahead of himself.

Way ahead.

Because he wanted a hell of a lot more from Lucy Dare than her body. That kiss had cemented her fate, just as it had shaken him to the very depths of his being. The minute his lips had hit hers, a jolt of awareness had struck him, more meaningful than lust. A sense of rightness had filled him, and every reason he shouldn't have tried to build a life with a good woman who, in Max's eyes, was nothing more than a pale imitation of the real thing had hit him hard.

Their four-year age difference didn't deter him either. Lucy had recently turned twenty-eight, but she was an old soul, forced to face life's harsh realities too young, as Max had been around to witness.

Max had been close to his parents when he was younger. They'd lived in a two-bedroom apartment, and his parents had worked hard at their restaurant business. When one of the restaurants had succeeded, they'd moved into the Dares' upper-middle-class neighborhood. His father had no longer needed his mother at work, and she'd turned her attention to her original love—social work. She'd gone on to make them an oddity in town by bringing in troubled foster kids—on whom they lavished love and caring, because *these children need it, Maximillian. You already have everything.*

Except the kind of attention they'd denied him. Not many of his foster siblings had wanted to hang out with the *rich kid*, as they'd called him, so Max had latched on to the Dare family. Back then he'd considered Lucy a pain in the ass who trailed after her brothers and him.

And then Lucy's parents had passed away, and Max had come home from college to find that a sad, quiet girl had replaced the vibrant one who'd loved to drive them all crazy. He'd become more protective of her then. And when she'd graduated from college, Max had taken one look at the curvy, adult, gorgeous woman she'd become . . . and he'd been transfixed.

At that point, the age difference would have driven the Dare brothers insane. He'd seen Decklan and Gabe chase away too many men interested in their sister to think otherwise. They wanted her to have the chance to live a full, exciting life. And at twenty-six, Max had already closed his heart to the idea of any emotional connection with a woman. Had he wanted a wife? Kids? Sure. But someone he loved with his whole heart, who could turn their backs on him the way his parents had? No, thank you.

Then he'd met Cindy, and they'd suited well enough, so he'd continued to date her seriously. As if on cue, Lucy had then moved to California. When she hadn't come to Max's wedding, he'd known then that he'd destroyed the bond they'd once shared. He'd told himself it was for the best. But he'd never put her out of his mind completely.

Still, Max's marriage had floundered, while Lucy, he knew from her brothers, had grown into an independent woman, and they were damned proud.

In the time since Cindy's passing, Max had grieved, suffered through self-imposed guilt for not being what she'd deserved. And he'd satisfied himself with one-night stands and weekends at Paradis in order to forget his mistakes and regrets. He'd grown up. And learned that his parents' failings and the fact that he'd nearly made similar mistakes couldn't define the rest of his life. He was ready for Lucy.

She was the one woman who could fit into his life and complete him in every way. Unlike her asshole ex-boyfriend, Max would never try to harness her vibrancy. She was a dynamo, and he wanted to feed off her energy and help her burn brighter. But to do that, he needed her closer to home. Closer to him. She just needed a reason . . . and Max had the perfect one to present to her.

But first, she had to return to the party.

"How'd it go, hotshot?" Decklan asked, approaching him with his fiancée, Amanda, by his side.

"Hey, gorgeous," Max said to the curvy blonde, who was positively beaming. "If this guy ever blows it, you give me a call." He winked at her and stepped back before Decklan could haul off and punch him.

"Ignoring my question?" Decklan asked.

"Leave Max alone," Amanda chided, curling herself around her fiancé as she spoke.

"Listen to your better half," Max said with an easy grin. But inside he wasn't smiling, and he turned to his best friend. "Listen up. From this moment on, whatever happens or doesn't happen between your sister and me is off-limits. As in none of your business."

Amanda sucked in a surprised breath. "You and Lucy?" she asked. "But I thought she was here with someone."

"He's gone," Max told her before glancing back at his best friend. "Understand?"

"Hell no. My sister, my business."

"My love life, *my* business," Max said, then mentally reassessed that statement. "My woman, my business."

"What do you mean, her boyfriend is gone?" Amanda asked, concerned.

Before any of them could continue, Max caught sight of Lucy *finally* making her way across the lawn. Her hair was still down, long and flowing, causing his fingers to itch with the need to slide through those thick strands again. Next time, he'd tug a bit harder and see how she responded to a bite of pain and command. His cock twitched in agreement.

"Lucy!" Amanda called her over.

Lucy met Max's gaze and tipped her chin a bit higher as she joined them.

"Hi. Enjoying your party?" she asked Amanda, ignoring Max.

So she was still mad at him, but she obviously wasn't about to avoid him. That was the woman he admired.

"I'm having the best time. It was a great idea to have an engagement party for friends, so just family can escape for the wedding next week," Amanda said, clearly excited.

The wedding itself would be an intimate destination affair on the island of Eden, consisting of Decklan's older brother, Gabe, and his wife, Isabelle, Max, and Lucy. If nothing else, their trip to Eden would give him a chance to seduce her in private.

Decklan pulled Amanda close, kissing her on the lips. "I can't wait to make this beautiful woman my wife. It's been too long a wait."

Lucy smiled wistfully at her brother, and Max caught the flash of pain in her expression before she vanquished it.

But Max had her all figured out. He ought to, considering her issues basically mirrored his. Fear of loss and abandonment. He knew it well. Had been force-fed it by Daniel Carver, his psychiatrist pal.

Lucy was happy for her brother, but with another one marrying, she was building up her walls even more, deliberately making herself the outsider in a family that only wanted to pull her in and keep her close. The New York Dare siblings were tight, and the fact that Lucy still lived in LA had more to do with her fear of loss than the desire to remain in California.

As Gabe and Decklan formed their own families, Lucy drew further and further away. She came home less often. He understood her in a deep way because he *knew* her and because she engaged him on a fundamental level he'd been forced to ignore. Until now.

"Hi, all," Gabe said as they widened their circle to include both him and Isabelle.

"Iz, thank you for letting me use your makeup earlier. I needed a touch-up." Lucy blushed, deliberately not meeting Max's gaze.

He caught Decklan's stunned expression as he probably figured out why she'd needed to fix herself. Well, what had the man expected when he'd given Max free reign?

"What's mine is yours," Isabelle said. "We're sisters, after all." She squeezed Lucy's hand.

"I wish you lived in New York," Isabelle said.

"I know, but my career is in LA."

"Is it?" Gabe asked, pinning his sister with a knowing stare.

Max picked up on his opening. "My understanding is that all the Elite clubs have been remodeled, and you have no new ones in the works."

Lucy shot him a nasty glare.

"True," Gabe said.

"Well, I can use Lucy in New York."

"What?" Lucy's wide-eyed gaze finally met his.

He grinned at the panic in her voice. "For business, princess." And more, but she wasn't ready to hear that yet.

The idea had come to him while thinking about her earlier. Max was a restaurateur with a brand-new project on the horizon. He also understood how tricky it was to nail ambience. People were fickle, and it was difficult if not damned near impossible to satisfy everyone, which was why New York City alone boasted an over eighty percent fail rate. New restaurants shut down within five years of opening. Nightclubs were no different.

"The designer I used on my other restaurants recently suffered a bout of debilitating Lyme disease. She's basically bedridden."

Lucy and the rest of them winced. "I hope she's okay."

"It's going to be a slow recovery. I need someone with your expertise to run with the new project."

He knew what she'd done with all the Elite clubs, and Lucy had more than proven her ability. She had an innate sense of what worked. She might be able to fight their sexual attraction and put up emotional walls, but she couldn't turn down a career-boosting opportunity. And what Max had in mind could put her on the map, opening up new avenues with big clientele.

He turned to face her, feeling a little bad at the wary, doe-in-the-headlights look in her eyes. But when he decided he wanted something, Max pulled out all the stops.

"Lucy, how would you like to design the next Max Savage restaurant in lower Manhattan?" he asked in his smoothest voice.

Lucy had never considered herself fragile. No matter what life threw at her, she'd always pulled herself together and moved on. But in this moment, she'd reached the limit of what she could handle.

Traveling to New York while listening to Lucas complain about missing meetings and work. Feeling the obvious tension and dislike her brothers had for her boyfriend and pasting a smile on her face anyway, because she wouldn't let anything ruin Decklan and Amanda's celebration. Max confronting her about her choice in men—her blood still boiled at that one—and that kiss . . . oh, that kiss . . . Then the argument and breakup with Lucas that she hadn't explained to anyone yet.

Now Max was offering her a job that required her to uproot her life in LA and return to her family's orbit . . . and Max's undeniable pull? Move to New York? Work with Max? Her heart beat harder at the thought, and panic set in.

Hell no, she thought.

"I think it's a fabulous idea!" Gabe said.

"Of course you do," she said under her breath.

Ignoring her, he went on. "You could move into my old apartment. I haven't sold it yet." Gabe took over, making decisions for her as was his MO. Another reason living in LA worked for her.

Lucy glared at Max for bringing up this idea in front of her siblings. "This is all very sudden," she said. "I can't just decide to move in an instant."

"But you aren't totally against the idea?" Decklan asked, excited at the prospect.

Max, *damn him*, just stared steadily at her, as if he could get his way by sheer force of will.

"She has a boyfriend in LA," Isabelle reminded Decklan. "You can't push her like that."

"Where is jerk-face anyway?" Gabe asked.

"Actually, Max said he left. He just didn't explain why." Decklan glanced at Lucy. "So answer Gabe's question. Where is jerk-face?"

She narrowed her gaze, and her palm twitched with the urge to smack him. If her brother wasn't careful, he'd give her the excuse she needed to blow off steam.

"Decklan," she said, definite warning in her tone. She wasn't ready for a general announcement about her love life. Especially one that would include her explaining how she'd kissed Max.

"Back off, boys." Isabelle stepped forward and grabbed Lucy's hand. "It's time for girl talk. Amanda? Inside, now." And just like that, Isabelle herded the women into the house.

"What about your guests?" Lucy asked as she followed her sister-in-law into her private study, where she shut the French doors behind them.

"The men can handle them. I'm worried about you, and that's all that matters right now."

Lucy glanced at her sister-in-law. Her long blonde hair curled around her shoulders, and her curvy body had only grown fuller postpregnancy, but what always struck Lucy about Isabelle was her warm, expressive features and caring nature. Suddenly overcome, she hugged the other woman tight, embarrassed when tears formed in her eyes.

"This is supposed to be Amanda's day, and here I am ruining it with drama."

"You couldn't ruin my day if you tried," Amanda said. She, like Isabelle, had blonde hair, though she had more waves than curls. And she also had a sweet, caring personality.

Her brothers had chosen well.

Lucy needed a tissue. Since becoming a mom, Isabelle had begun to stock every room with toddler necessities. A quick glance, and she found a box on the desk. She pulled one out and blotted her eyes.

"Now what can we do to help? Because I didn't mean to give Max an opening about the job. Is that what this is about?" Amanda asked.

"It's a lot of things." *Beginning and ending with Max*, Lucy thought.

"Let's begin with the fact that Lucas is gone?" Isabelle asked.

"Right. That's because we're over," Lucy admitted.

Both women gasped in startled surprise. "What happened?" Amanda asked. "I mean, he looked preoccupied . . ."

"And I saw him sitting in his car on the phone earlier," Isabelle added.

"Max kissed me, I kissed him back, and nothing's been right since," Lucy said in one big confessional rush.

"No way!" Amanda said.

"It's about time," Isabelle said pointedly.

Lucy frowned at her. "Really? You're going to side with him? First, he all but called Lucas a jackass—"

"Which he is." Before Isabelle could say more, sweet babbling noises sounded from the baby monitor hooked to her waist.

"Do you need to get to Noah?" Lucy asked hopefully. She adored her nephew, even if he did have his daddy's stubborn tilt to his chin and determination to get his way. He'd be a true Dare man, Lucy thought.

Isabelle grinned. "No such luck. That's his happy, *I'm talking to my giraffe, don't bother me* sound. Now is Max the reason Lucas left?"

Lucy rubbed her hands up and down her arms. "I asked Lucas to come back inside and really get to know my family, my brothers, and both of you . . ."

"You wanted him to get to know me?" Amanda asked.

"Of course. You're going to be my sister, and you make my brother so happy. You're family."

Amanda studied her through suddenly damp eyes.

Lucy blinked. "What's wrong?"

"It's just that since we met, you've kept yourself apart from us. From me. I thought maybe you didn't like me or think I was good enough for your brother." Amanda's voice trembled as she spoke. "I tried to get to know you, to push a little, but it's hard for me. And . . . I'm so glad I read you wrong." Amanda wrapped her arms around Lucy.

The hug reinforced the guilt Lucy was feeling. She'd been so worried about keeping her own emotions safe that she'd made Amanda feel bad about herself and neglected the people she cared about the most. Decklan had explained to Lucy about Amanda's insecurities thanks to her bitch of a mother, and the last thing she wanted to do was reinforce any of them.

"I'm sorry," Lucy murmured. "It's not you. I'm really not as together as I like people to think."

Isabelle laughed. "None of us are, which is why Amanda and I understand you better than you realize."

Lucy nodded. She knew both women had their own issues, their own stories as they'd struggled through falling in love with her brothers.

"So what happened?" Isabelle asked, her pit bull nature coming through.

Lucy leaned against the desk, easing one hip down. "Lucas took a look at me, realized I wasn't as put together as I was when we arrived, and I confessed." She waved her hands in the air as she explained. "He called me a whore and a tramp, Max stepped in and threatened to spread his teeth across the street, and Lucas took off." Lucy managed a shaky laugh. "It has been one hell of a day," she muttered.

"And then Max offered you a job," Amanda said, summing up her newest problem. "Are you going to take it?"

"I think you should at least consider it," Isabelle said, surprising Lucy.

"Seriously?"

"At least the part about coming home. You don't have to work for him if you don't want to—although there's so much potential for you if you do take the job . . . in more ways than one." She wagged her eyebrows in an obvious reference to Lucy and Max hooking up.

Lucy shot her a dirty look.

"She didn't say *take* the job, she said consider it," Amanda added in an attempt to be helpful.

"Right. Consider it. Then accept." Isabelle grinned. "Don't you want to be around to see your nephew grow up? And on that parting note, I hear my baby calling me." She patted the silent monitor on her hip.

"Liar," Lucy muttered.

With a wink, Isabelle walked out the door, and Lucy heard her footsteps as she ran up the stairs toward her one-year-old's room.

Amanda met Lucy's gaze and shrugged. "Umm, I ought to get back to the party."

Another traitor, Lucy thought. But she didn't want to upset Amanda so soon after her admission about thinking Lucy didn't like her when nothing could be further from the truth.

"Go ahead. I'll be out in a few minutes." Lucy wanted some time to pull her thoughts together before facing her brothers . . . or Max.

She wasn't ready to decide about her future just yet. With the destination wedding around the corner, she'd been planning on making the nearby hotel room her home base until she returned from Eden. But now that she was alone, she might as well be comfortable while in New York, and her brother's awesome place in Manhattan was perfect. She already had her own room there anyway, with extra clothes and toiletries and makeup.

The sound of the doors slamming shut startled her, and she turned to find Max standing in the entry to the study. For the first time all day, she allowed herself to really look him over, without guilt, without shame.

His dirty-blond hair, always a touch too long, gave him a roguish look that appealed to her . . . despite her having dated clean-cut Lucas. Max might be a businessman, but muscles bulged beneath his cream-colored dress shirt, and masculinity exuded from every pore. His face was tanned and oh so handsome while his sexy white smile could make her panties melt away, and she shifted uncomfortably, not wanting him to notice how he affected her.

She straightened her posture and decided to get this discussion over with. "Max."

"The party is emptying out."

She released a breath she hadn't been aware of holding. "That's good. I'll just borrow Gabe's car, head on back to the hotel, and pick up my things."

Max shook his head. "You aren't going to face that asshole alone."

"You're the one who kissed his girlfriend. I'm sure *he* thinks you're the ass."

Max treated her to a wicked grin. "Fair point. I'm still not letting you deal with him by yourself."

"Let me?" Lucy's anger threatened to boil over. "You're not *letting* me?" she repeated, her voice rising. "Someone spare me from these alpha men in my life!"

"At least you admit I'm *in* your life."

Leave it to him to take her insult and turn it into an *in* of some kind. "I can drive myself to the hotel. Lucas was angry, but he won't hurt me."

"No, he'll just insult you," Max muttered. "You have two choices. You can let me drive you there, or I can ask one of your brothers to do it instead."

Gabe still had guests, and it was Decklan and Amanda's special day. Even so, either one of them would agree with Max and insist on driving her to the hotel. "You don't play fair."

"Never said I did." He walked over and placed a warm hand behind her back.

Her body, still on edge from that hot kiss and the desire he'd seamlessly ignited inside her earlier, trembled, his touch setting her on fire all over again.

"Lead the way," she said, her husky voice giving away too much. Max's ego was already big enough. He didn't need any more encouragement or incentive.

If Lucy knew Lucas, and she did, he'd packed up and headed for the airport to get on the next flight to LA. In all probability, he would be long gone by the time they arrived, making the trip to the hotel quick and painless. Or as painless as it could be with hot, gorgeous Max by her side.

At the hotel, Max was disappointed he didn't have the ex-boyfriend to deal with. Another lesson in how to treat a lady would have been a pleasure. Yes, he knew he'd provoked the man, and he shouldn't have pushed Lucy into that kiss, but regardless, Lucas's anger should have been directed at Max and never at Lucy.

She didn't speak to him while she packed up her things or during the drive to Manhattan. He didn't mind the silence, using the time instead to soak in her scent and just appreciate the fact that he finally could act on his desires. Once he had Lucy alone, he'd be a man on a mission, and she'd have his full attention.

At Gabe's, he insisted on carrying her bags, and they took the elevator up to the apartment on Fifth Avenue, overlooking Central Park. Max, too, lived on the Upper East Side, not far from here, which made Lucy's decision to stay in the city and not upstate even more convenient. Not that he'd tell her that. He had enough stacked against him as it was.

The doorman automatically let them up, and after more silence in the elevator, they stepped into the darkened hallway, and Lucy deactivated the alarm and unlocked the door.

He wheeled her large suitcase into the foyer and placed her carry-on on the floor beside it. "That's everything," he said.

She turned to him, meeting his gaze. "Thank you so much for helping me out," she said sweetly. "It was really nice of you to go out of your way."

He narrowed his gaze at her sudden sugary tone. She was up to something for sure. "Anything for you, princess. You don't know that yet, but you will."

"You do realize I just ended a long-term relationship, right? Add to that jetlag and exhaustion . . . I think I just need to get some sleep."

He grinned. Then he laughed.

"What's so funny?" She folded her arms across her chest, and he did his best not to ogle her cleavage, which protruded enticingly from behind the flimsy silk.

"You are. You really think you're getting rid of me that easily?"

"A girl can hope." She turned her back to him and headed inside the large apartment, her heels clicking along the marble floors.

Without waiting for an invitation that wouldn't be coming, Max grabbed her luggage and followed, catching up with her in the living room. "Want these in the master?" he asked.

She pursed her lips at him, then sighed. "No. I'll stay in the guest room. It already has all my things. First open doorway on the right," she said begrudgingly and gestured down the hall.

He entered the overly large bedroom suite with wall-to-wall windows on one side surrounded by light curtains and another set of huge windows on the adjoining wall. By the bed, Georgia O'Keefe paintings decorated the room, giving the space a bright, beautiful look. Pure Lucy.

"You decorated this," he said, knowing she'd followed him in. She stood in the doorway, watching him warily.

She inclined her head. "Gabe wanted me to be comfortable when I stayed here." She stepped inside and leaned against the nearest peach-colored wall.

Her guard was up, but he'd expected that. "I'd bet you decorated the whole apartment."

"Good guess."

"Not a guess. It has your signature lightness," he explained. He'd known the first time he visited that the place had Lucy's touch.

A flash of appreciation flickered across her face. "You noticed."

"I notice everything about you, Lucy." He stalked toward her, intent on making a point. "Just because I never acted on it before doesn't mean I wasn't completely aware." He cornered her between his body and the wall, inhaling her scent.

She trembled, as visibly affected by his nearness as he was by hers. "Max," she whispered.

Her soft skin beckoned to him, and he ran a finger down her cheek. It took all his willpower to hold back from taking things further, from picking her up and tying her to that frilly bed so she couldn't run from her own feelings. Instead, he knew he had to give her time.

"Don't worry," he assured her. "We're going to take it slow." It might kill him, but he'd get her to the point where she could face her feelings and fears. And he'd be there with her every step of the way.

"To start with, I'm going to send you information on the location for Savage in SoHo."

Her eyes lit up, giving him hope she'd take the job. "Are you going to tell me about your chef?"

"Sebastian Del Toro." He couldn't help the grin on his face as he told her.

"He came in second on the *Cooking Competition* show this past summer!"

"That's him," Max said.

She'd watched the show often, enjoying all the antics of the cast. "He would have come in first if they could have proved the guy in first place cheated, right?"

Max nodded.

"That is amazing! How'd you snag him? I read that everyone was trying to lure him in."

"Turns out we go way back. I know him from college." They were close friends; both shared a love of the food industry and had stayed in touch. "He's talented and deserved to win. But then he'd be running a different New York restaurant and not coming to work for me. And I'm a guaranteed success."

She shook her head and grinned. "I'm really impressed. This restaurant is going to be a hit."

Max nodded because he agreed and was pleased she saw things his way. "I'll forward you the information so you can see the vision Sebastian and I share. That way you can decide if the project excites you."

"You excite me," Lucy said, her eyes widening as the words escaped.

Max barely refrained from capturing her lips at her unbidden proclamation. But he hadn't gotten where he was after buying out his parents' restaurants by ignoring the bigger picture. Sex wasn't what he wanted from Lucy. His throbbing cock disagreed, and he amended the thought. Sex wasn't only what he wanted from Lucy.

"I'd be happy to look over the proposal," she finally said.

"I'll have my assistant send over a package tomorrow."

"Okay," she said, her warm breath fanning over his face, testing his restraint.

He nodded and stepped back, his body and mind protesting him leaving her when everything in him wanted to stay. If he walked away now, she'd think about what didn't happen between them. Longing and desire would fill her mind, and hopefully she'd toss and turn, wishing she'd acted on her needs. But if he kissed her, she'd fill her head with more anger and regret and push him away.

Decision made, he dragged himself away. "Lock up behind me."

"It's a security building, but don't worry. I will." She followed him to the door, her uncertainty at what he'd do next painfully obvious.

"Sweet dreams," he said before forcing his legs to move and leave her alone in that big, empty apartment. But before she closed the door, he didn't miss the disappointment that crossed her pretty face.

Between last-minute bridesmaid dress fittings, a spa/bonding day with Amanda and Isabelle, and going through the information Max had sent over about his new restaurant, Lucy's week before the wedding trip to Eden was busy. She shouldn't have had much time to think about her future, let alone dwell on her feelings for Max. Yet somehow, that's all she did.

One would think that she'd spend time mourning a relationship of almost a year or that she'd try to make sense out of how things had ended with Lucas. Instead, she accepted the outcome and let it go easily. Max consumed her thoughts, her days, and her nights.

Yet since he'd walked out the door, she hadn't heard a personal word from the man. Apparently when he said he intended to take things slow, he meant it. Or maybe he'd changed his mind completely, and she didn't like how that made her feel. She shouldn't want him so badly, but she did. But she wouldn't be the one to break down and call him. She'd see him on the island along with the rest of her family.

On travel day, she woke up with a mixture of excitement and trepidation swirling inside her. Her brother was getting married on the fantastical, magical island of Eden, where anything could happen and often did. And Lucy had no idea what, if anything, Max had planned.

Chapter Three

*L*ucy flew from New York to Miami for the trip to Eden with more than normal travel butterflies in her stomach. She was a pro at flying coast to coast, but the Eden trip was different. As she'd experienced during the construction and opening of Eden Elite, their most exclusive resort worldwide, the second leg of the trip to the island was on a tiny prop plane that took off from Miami, Florida.

Although Joely, the pilot, was experienced, small planes made Lucy nervous. Her parents had died in a car crash, and the loud sounds and enclosed space inside the little aircraft always made her think about her parents' last minutes on earth. Not pleasant thoughts, and not ones she cared to repeat today. Still, for Decklan and Amanda, she'd endure.

The soon-to-be married couple had flown out earlier in the week, while Gabe and Isabelle were arriving tomorrow. She comforted herself with the thought that once she arrived at the gorgeous resort, she'd have four long days of bliss, fun . . . and Max.

"Lucy!"

She turned at the sound of her name to see Joely waving to her from the tarmac. She walked out of the building and met her on the runway, the white plane with the red stripe in the background.

"It's so good to see you again!"

The petite woman hugged her warmly. "So let's get you to the island. Our other passenger is already on board."

"Other passenger?" Lucy asked, but Joely had already started for the aircraft, and Lucy had a good idea who waited inside.

She drew a deep breath and walked up the boarding steps, not surprised when she found Max grinning inside. "Well, hello there."

Her breath caught at the sight of him. Max was stunning in his normal business attire, dress slacks and a button-down shirt, like he'd worn at the engagement party. The casually dressed man lounging in his seat took her breath away. A pair of khaki cargo shorts showed off his strong, toned, and tanned legs. A faded, wrinkled Life is Good T-shirt in sea green accented his eyes. The boating shoes were so un-Max-like that she had to suppress a smile.

Unshaven, a baseball cap turned backward on his head, he was the epitome of the bad boy she remembered from her youth. The one who'd driven her teenage hormones insane and was now making her adult female parts zing like crazy.

She took the only empty seat—next to him, of course—and set her bag at her feet. "I didn't know you were on this flight."

He shrugged. "I wasn't sure I'd make it. I flew down to check on a problem at the Miami restaurant . . . and I had some personal things to take care of so I could be totally free. For you." She narrowed her gaze, sensing something extremely serious in his tone and meaning. "Luckily for me, the timing worked. So here I am."

"Lucky me," she said warily as she slid her seat belt closed.

A few minutes later, the doors shut tight, and Joely took off. The roar of the engines surrounded her, and Lucy clasped her hands in her lap, reminding herself that the flight would be over before she knew it. She just had to keep her irrational fears in check.

She drew deep breaths, counting in and out, to ten and back, seeking calm. And praying Max would close his eyes and ignore her ridiculous reaction to the flight.

Max glanced down at Lucy's fingers, twisted so tightly that the tips were practically white from pressure and lack of circulation.

He covered her hands with his larger one. "Hey. We're safe. And it's a short trip."

"I know. I've made this trip many times, remember?"

He didn't buy the flippant answer. "Then what's got you so stressed out?" He brushed his thumb over the soft skin on her hand.

She blew out a long breath, her glossed lips puckering in a way that had his own mouth watering. He was dying to taste her again, to nibble on those luscious lips and make her forget all about whatever was bothering her.

Instead, he grasped her chin and turned her to face him. Her dark-blue eyes were wide and filled with fear. "Lucy?"

"Do you think my parents knew?" she asked. "At the end, I mean? Or do you think they were just here and then . . . gone?" The question took him off guard.

It was one he'd asked himself many times about Cindy, who'd ironically died the same way. Except Lucy's parents had been in a torrential rainstorm, and Cindy hadn't been. It was the last topic he'd have thought was on her mind now.

"I wish I had an answer," he said honestly. "But I don't. I do, however, understand why you wonder."

She winced. "I'm sorry. I forgot your . . . wife"—she choked over the word—"died the same way. That was insensitive of me."

"It's okay." Cindy was a subject they'd have to discuss at some point . . . but they were a long way from that day. "I never realized you being in this tin can would bring back those memories."

She sniffed, the tip of her nose turning red. "I try not to think about it often, but yeah. In here, it always comes back."

"Why didn't you fly out with Decklan and Amanda? Or wait for Gabe and Isabelle?" He hesitated before adding, "Or ask me what flight I was taking?"

"I need to know I can survive these things alone."

He appreciated the fact that she confided in him, and as always, he admired her strength. But her words confounded him. "Hmm."

"What's that for?"

"You didn't say you need to do these things on your own, but that you need to *survive* them. It just strikes me," he said carefully, knowing that picking into her mind could cause her to withdraw, "that it's a drastic way of looking at things. Just like I think moving and staying in California is a drastic way of protecting yourself from being hurt."

She narrowed her gaze. "When did you become a psychologist?"

He shrugged. "Trust me, in the last four years, I've had a lot of time to analyze my actions and to think. So yeah, I like to think I know what I'm talking about."

He paused for a moment, then continued. "Just ask yourself one thing. If something suddenly happened to one of your brothers, like it did to your parents, would living so far away really protect you from pain? Or would you regret not soaking up all the time with them you could have beforehand?"

She opened her mouth to answer, probably to rip into him, and then turbulence hit. The plane bounced repeatedly. He grabbed the armrest and held on. If they hadn't been seat belted, they'd have been seriously jostled around inside the plane.

"Hang on, folks," Joely called over her shoulder. "I just need to bring us to a higher altitude for a less bumpy ride."

Max clamped his hand over Lucy's. A glance told him she'd gone pale. "Did I ever tell you I'm afraid of roller coasters?" he asked.

"Liar." The corners of her mouth turned up slightly, and he considered it a victory.

The plane jolted so hard, he felt it in the pit of his stomach.

"Just a tropical storm that came in fast. I'll get us out," Joely said from the front of the plane, her voice a calm promise.

But the wild look in Lucy's eyes didn't abate.

"Stay with me, princess," Max murmured.

She blinked and nodded, but her breathing came in shorter and shorter pants, so Max did the only thing he could to distract her. He leaned over and kissed her.

The edge of the seat belt dug into his stomach, and he didn't give a damn. The only thing that mattered was Lucy, and her taste was like a drug. One kiss the other day hadn't been enough. He'd been craving her ever since.

Now he had her.

He teased her, gliding his tongue across the seam of her lips, then thrusting inside the moment she parted for him. She tasted like coffee and mint, and as his tongue swept through the dark recesses of her mouth, his body burned with want. His goal was to keep her focus on him and not the bumpy ride, but she shot his concentration straight to hell, and all he could think about was *more*.

He cupped her face in his hand and tilted her head, keeping her in place as he swirled his tongue around and around, drinking her in. She whimpered under his assault, her body softening as she leaned closer, accepting what he offered, kissing him back.

"We're out of the storm, lovebirds," Joely called out cheerfully.

Max cursed the pilot under his breath and treated himself to another longer, more thorough taste of Lucy before forcing himself to pull back.

Lucy stared at him, dazed. "You kissed me again."

"Kept you from panicking," he said, then, not wanting her to yell at him or set boundaries he'd have every intention of crossing, he changed the subject. "So did you read over the information on Savage in SoHo? Damn, I love that name, don't you?"

"Nice ego." Her navy eyes flickered in amusement, and her tongue swiped over her lips. Lips damp from his kiss. He shifted in his seat.

"Yes, I've read through everything, and I love the tapas concept," she said, relaxing into her seat. "I still can't believe you snagged Sebastian Del Toro."

He was damned proud of the fact that he had. Friendship or not, Sebastian had other choices.

"How'd you manage it?" she asked. "Was it just the friendship?"

"Hell no." Max folded his arms across his chest. "I made him an offer he couldn't refuse."

She rolled her eyes. "You aren't the godfather."

"No, but I offered him all the control he wanted. You see, the one thing I've learned is that as long as I can control the business end of things, giving my creative types the illusion of control everywhere else makes them happy. In other words, I get what I want." He held her gaze for another beat.

She shivered, and he knew she got the meaning behind his words.

"I hear they call him the playboy chef. Any truth to the rumors?" she asked.

Max groaned. She'd just hit on the one drawback to hiring Sebastian. "They're true. He actually got caught fucking one of the stagehands. The only reason they kept him on the show was because of the great arguments between him and Anthony Abbadon. The ratings were too high, so they gave him a stern warning, and the show went on. Lost his current girlfriend in the process. Not that he treats any woman well enough for them to stick around, but I hear this one was in for the long haul. She made a huge scene and got herself thrown off the lot where they were shooting." Max shook his head. "Damned eccentric and temperamental chefs," he muttered. And he ought to know, because he had to work with them.

He glanced out the window just as a stone castle came into view. Rumor had it the owner of the island and resort had imported the building directly from Ireland. With the sun lighting up the sky behind it, the castle presented a beautiful, if imposing, view.

"Feel better?" he asked her.

She tucked a strand of hair behind her ear and nodded. "If you're asking me if your distraction worked, the answer is yes." Her cheeks flushed pink at the reminder.

Or should he say, turned pinker? Her skin was still as rosy from that kiss as he was hard inside his shorts. "Then take a look outside."

He pointed to the incredible landscape of the island itself, the sky varying shades of blue, the clouds pure white, no sign of the storm that had frightened her.

"Oh, Max."

He wanted to hear that sound while his dick was buried deep inside her soft flesh. He shook his head hard to dislodge the visual.

"No matter how many times I come here, the view always captivates me," she said in awe. "Speaking of, did you know the island is reported to hold magical qualities? Because it's located near the Bermuda Triangle. Visitors claim their wishes and dreams have been answered here," Lucy said.

"Come on." Max cocked an eyebrow. He'd heard mumbo jumbo about the island, but he didn't believe in magic.

"It's true," Joely said, joining the conversation. "People who come here always leave changed in some way."

Max didn't have time to answer or think more. Joely brought them to a smooth landing, and before they knew it, they deplaned, their pilot insisting all their bags would be brought to their rooms.

"Wait until you see the rooms here," Lucy said, her eyes lighting with excitement. "They're so luxurious . . . and the view is incredible."

Max nodded. The view would be incredible, all right. It just wouldn't be the view she thought.

As soon as Lucy set foot on the island, the scent of salt water mixed with island flowers assaulted her senses. The sun blazed overhead, and all the tension in her muscles drained away as her body recognized the relaxation represented by the smells and sights around her. That sense of calm didn't last long.

The last few times she'd been to Eden, Lucy had walked up the stone pathway and stairs, ending up in the main hotel, but now she found herself riding in a golf cart driven by a hotel employee . . . and sitting way too close to Max. His masculine scent overrode all the other island aromas, working her body into a heated frenzy. It was almost as if being on the island had turned her awareness of him into overdrive.

She forced herself to focus on the foliage-laced path that led to the beach instead of on him. "Where are we going?" she asked. "Because I know the hotel is in the other direction."

"Patience, Grasshopper," Max said.

She shot him a dirty look. "I don't like surprises."

"I figured that out," he said, looking mighty pleased with himself.

"And you don't know the island, so what gives?"

He leaned an arm behind her and turned, his strong, bare thighs aligning with hers. The short sundress had clearly been a bad idea, allowing for way too much body contact.

"We're staying in a bungalow on the water," he said.

"We?"

"That's what you took from my explanation? You've got four sun-filled days directly on the beach, and you're worried about who's staying where?"

"We can't be staying together." Her heart fluttered in panic at the thought.

"Actually, we're in the same bungalow, but there are separate rooms."

She shook her head. "No. My brothers wouldn't have booked me in a cabin with you."

"You're right. They didn't. This is my way of making sure we get alone time." He smiled, his teeth white against his tanned skin, his grin extra sexy. "Now take a deep breath, chill, and enjoy the scenery."

She tried. Gripping the side of the cart hard, she breathed in the warm, humid air, exhaled slowly . . . and asked herself why she was still fighting him so hard.

She was single. So was he. She was beyond attracted to him, and this trip presented her with the chance to get Max out of her system once and for all.

As for her fears, Lucy wasn't looking to get attached, and by his behavior and history, neither was Max. He'd married once, true, but not only had his wife passed away—according to Decklan, there'd been issues between them. Cindy had wanted more than Max had been willing to give. And in the years since, he'd never had a serious relationship. In fact, she knew he'd frequented the same sex club Decklan and Amanda had, something she tried not to think about too hard. Because why would she want to know about her brother's sex life? And because the notion of Max in leather pants, exercising his strong will over her, appealed to her. Too much.

She still couldn't believe he'd changed up their accommodations for the wedding weekend. "My brothers won't kill you for this move?"

"As a matter of fact, I have their approval," he said, his voice smug.

"Seriously?"

"I'm a good guy, and they know it."

Lucy couldn't help it. She snorted in laughter. "More like you box, and they know it."

"I'm sure it helps." Max folded his arms across his chest, flexing his ample muscles.

Her mouth watered, and she found herself unable to look away. He was toned, tanned, and so freaking good-looking. She'd be a fool to turn down what he was offering, something she wanted just as badly.

"Okay, Max. Guess what? I'll chill and enjoy what the island brings." And what happens on Eden stays on Eden.

She could live with that.

The look of surprise on his face pleased her. She liked taking him off guard for once.

The driver stopped in front of the cabin. There was a good distance between the bungalows on the beach, giving each privacy, but there were people within walking distance. Once their bags were inside, they were left alone. The cabin itself was small but clean and decorated with an easy beachy feel. No carpets that would get mildewed from the sand and water, light wood furnishings, and a fully stocked kitchen.

Lucy knew there were restaurants at the main hotel and room service wherever and whenever you wanted to be served. The island catered to comfort and amenities, and she loved it here.

The two bedrooms were identical, and she unpacked in one. Since it was just a little after noon, she had the whole day ahead of her and changed into her favorite bathing suit, a lavender bikini that showed off a lot of skin. If she had to face Max, she was glad she'd taken the time to work out at the gym back in LA.

She walked through the cabin and out onto the deck, looking over at the glistening blue water in the near distance, and sighed in pleasure. The quiet struck her immediately. It was so peaceful here.

"Where are the other guests?" she asked aloud.

"I don't know. I requested seclusion."

Max's husky voice sounded from behind her, and she trembled at the low tenor of his voice. "You were very sure of yourself," she said as she turned to face him.

"Not really." His cocky façade cracked for a moment, and she saw the uncertainty in his gaze. "I want you, Lucy. All I can do is show you how much." He stepped closer, his hands grasping the railing as he bracketed her against the porch.

She raised her hands to his bare chest, her palms against his warm skin. "If you want me, come get me," she said in a teasing tone, then pushed him away. Using the element of surprise, she ducked around him and ran for the water.

Struck by her sudden playfulness, Max took off after her, his gaze on her sexy curves and tanned skin as she ran. He reached out, intending to wrap his arm around her waist and pull her against him before she reached the water, but he missed a full-body grab and ended up pulling the back string on her bikini top instead.

She spun around at the same time her top dropped down, revealing her bare breasts to the sun and his heated gaze. Dusky nipples and creamy white skin had his mouth watering. He was dying to pull one of the tight buds into his mouth and suckle hard until she was squirming and begging for relief.

Before he could move too far too fast, he scooped her up in his arms and kept heading for the water, hoping it was freaking cold enough to cool him down. Because one look at her sexy tits, and he was hard as a rock and ready to blow.

"Max!" she squealed and wrapped her legs tight around his waist, which did nothing to help his current state of arousal.

His legs hit the *warm* water. *So much for relief,* he thought wryly. Torturing himself further, he slid her down the length of his body, her hard nipples grazing his chest until her feet hit the water.

"I'm glad you're in a playful mood, princess."

"I decided to enjoy what the island has to offer."

"The island? Or me?" he asked.

"You, Max." She threaded her fingers through his hair, her nails scraping along his scalp. He barely managed to stifle a groan. "While we're here, I'm yours."

Her words stunned him, and though he didn't like the time limit she set, he wasn't about to turn his back on a gift he wanted badly. He preferred to look at it as time to convince her of how good they could be together.

"But I am going to make you work for it." Laughing and not the least bit self-conscious about being naked on top, she dove beneath the blue water.

He shook his head and went after her. What ensued was reminiscent of when they were kids—a water fight, splashing and all. Except this time, they weren't children. By the time she ran out of steam, she came up from the water like a mermaid rising from the ocean. Head tipped back, she brushed her hair away from her face, her perky nipples pointing skyward, as she'd long since lost the bikini top to the waves. Playtime was over.

Their play had ratcheted up his desire, and he hooked a foot around her leg, causing her to trip forward. He caught her as she crashed against him, sliding his hands up her naked back, tracing the bones along her spine. She arched into him, purring like a cat.

He couldn't resist and tipped her face up, kissing her salty lips and sliding his hands up her tapered waist, brushing his thumbs beneath her breasts, feeling her desire swell as her nipples puckered into his chest. He drank from her mouth, and she let him, opening, meeting his tongue thrust for thrust, swept away in the passion they generated. And this time, she wasn't pulling back. Instead, she was rocking herself against him, her soft sighs and moans lost inside his mouth. He breathed her air; she inhaled his. Grabbing her ass in his hands, he pressed her lithe body into him, letting her feel his hunger for her.

She broke the kiss, gasping for much-needed air. "Max, please." Her hips gyrated against his, and he understood what she was asking for. A glance around the sandy beach told him they were still very much alone. He could draw out her pleasure and luxuriate in all that was Lucy.

She wanted relief. He wanted time.

"First things first." He reached for her breasts, cupping them in his hands. They were small but made to fit in his palms. "I've waited a long time to see you like this . . . my big hands on your fucking perfect breasts." He palmed each, then moved to her nipples, plucking them with his fingertips. "Let's find out how sensitive you are."

She moaned at the idea, and when he squeezed her nipple hard, she leaned against him, her soft body cushioned against him as he continued to play. Her sighs and the shifting of her body showed him how responsive she was and it worked him into a state.

He gritted his teeth and slid his hand into the band of her bikini bottoms, coming into contact with smooth, bare skin.

He sucked in a shallow breath, his cock very much aware of the fact that he wouldn't be the one getting relief. And he didn't care.

"Hold on to me," he instructed, and she responded immediately, grasping his forearms tightly. Her sex was slick with arousal, his fingers drenched. "You're so wet," he said, a low groan of satisfaction ripping from his throat.

"Are you going to do something about it?" she asked.

At her teasing attempt at control, he squeezed one ass cheek in his hand. She gasped, her blue eyes opening wide, followed by a renewed wetness coating his fingers.

"I will when you let me call the shots." He watched her carefully. Normally, Lucy would give him hell about his need to dominate, but right now? Her blue eyes softened, and she spread her legs wider and waited.

He loved that his gut was right, that she would like submitting in the bedroom. Inside and out, she'd push his boundaries too, and damned if he didn't get off on that. Right now, though, his focus was on getting *her* off.

He kissed her cheek, slid his tongue along her soft jawline and down her neck. Her head tipped back to give him better access.

"Mmm, that feels good," she murmured. "You feel good."

He nipped at her jaw. "And you taste delicious," he murmured, tasting the salt on her skin. He was more than happy to make a meal of her right here and now.

Meanwhile, his fingers worked her sex, sliding back and forth across her soft, slick flesh, and he clenched his jaw against the sensations rocking his body at the feel of her juices and heat. He kept up the pressure and rubbed his fingers along her slit, spreading the moisture around before pressing his finger directly on her clit.

Her hips bucked, and she began circling against his hand. He dipped lower, easing one finger inside her while continuing to stimulate her clit with his thumb. It didn't take long before he found the spot inside her that, combined with the insistent external pressure, had her coming apart in his arms. And what a sight it was, the sun on her face, her body flush against his, trembling as her lips parted with pleasure *he* was giving.

He held her until she came back to herself, then, without a word, scooped her into his arms and carried her back to the bungalow. They'd had fun. And she'd come hard. Mission one accomplished.

Chapter Four

*L*ucy showered, aware that Max was in the next room, probably doing the same thing. Her body still tingled from that amazing orgasm, yet funny enough, her climax wasn't the main thing that struck her about today. She'd spent so long changing and muting herself to suit someone else's needs, she'd surprised herself with her game of catch me if you can. They'd played in the ocean, splashing and frolicking, both well aware of the sexual undercurrents between them. It had been a very long time since Lucy had allowed herself to relax and enjoy life. Too long, if her enjoyment and reaction to today was any indication.

Knowing her tendency to peel from sunburn, she slathered her body in coconut moisturizer before pulling on a white sundress that tied like a halter on top. She knew too well what had happened the last time she'd worn a string tie around Max. Her nipples were deliciously sore from his calloused fingertips, and her sex still felt achy and wet. Shower or not, just thinking of Max got her juices flowing all over again.

She drew a deep breath and walked into the living area, where Max was pouring himself a glass of Avión tequila on the rocks. His bare feet peeked out of a faded pair of jeans. He hadn't yet put on a shirt, and his hair was still damp from the shower. He was muscular, masculine, and hot. She was dying to lick every inch of that gorgeous body and let him do the same to her. Gone were her reservations when all that awaited her was fun and pleasure. She just needed to keep perspective, and she'd have the vacation of a lifetime.

He turned, as if he'd sensed her. "Hey, beautiful." His eyes roamed over her appreciatively. Again, it had been so long since any man had looked at her with such blatant longing and admiration for the woman she was, it was a heady feeling. And one she could get used to.

"Can I get you a drink?" he asked.

She nodded. "I'll have a glass of Chardonnay if we have it?"

He opened the small refrigerator in the bar area and pulled out a bottle. "Looks like we're well stocked."

He pulled out the cork and poured her a glass.

"Decklan called me while I was getting dressed. They wanted to join us for dinner, but Amanda isn't feeling well. They figure it's better she rest before the rehearsal and wedding." Lucy shook her head and sighed. "I feel so bad for her, going away for her wedding and ending up sick."

Max nodded. "Hopefully it's a twenty-four-hour thing and she'll feel better tomorrow. Although I can't say I'm disappointed to have you alone for the night."

Warmth settled in the pit of her stomach at his words. She eased into the soft, plush couch and curled her legs beneath her. "So what did you want to do for dinner? The main resort has a great restaurant, and there's also poolside dining."

Before he could answer, a knock sounded at the door. "I'll get it." Max strode over to the door and returned with a young woman dressed in the resort's standard khakis and white shirt, carrying in a tray of food.

She placed everything on the table in front of the couch as per Max's instructions. "Can I get you anything else?" she asked.

"No, thank you, we're good," Max said.

She smiled. "Enjoy."

"Thank you," Lucy said, surprised that Max had obviously thought ahead. Then again, he'd set up this beachfront bungalow for two, so nothing he planned ought to surprise her.

"What are we eating?" she asked.

"I thought we'd have drinks and appetizers here, and then if you wanted a more substantial meal, we could head up to the resort." He sat down beside her, stretching one arm behind her, then pulling her against him. "Or we could stay here for the night," he said in a gruff voice that left no doubt as to which choice he preferred.

He pressed a kiss to her temple, his lips warm, his touch both sweet and arousing at the same time.

"We'll see," she said playfully, knowing exactly what her body wanted, what she finally accepted she was ready for. She took a long sip of the velvety, rich wine before pulling the silver top off of the selection of hors d'oeuvres. "Oh, I love brie and crackers."

He immediately leaned forward and cut a small piece of cheese, placed it on a cracker, and held it out for her to taste, his gaze intent on hers. She opened her mouth, and he slid the cracker onto her tongue, his fingers trailing over her lower lip as he pulled away. Her body trembled at his deliberately sensual touch, her breasts heavy and tight, her sex wet and needy. She chewed the creamy, crunchy snack and moaned. "Delicious."

He cocked an eyebrow. "Is it? I wouldn't know."

She grinned and picked up a cracker, added a slice of brie, and lifted it toward him. He opened and pulled the food into his mouth along with her fingers, sliding his lips along her skin before releasing her with a pop. He grinned while chewing and swallowing.

"Good?" she asked.

"Mouthwatering," he said, sexy lips lifted in a seductive grin.

She laughed. Laughed! She'd done more laughing today than in the recent past. She bit down on her lower lip. Had her life been that boring? Routine, maybe. *No*, she thought, hating the admission. It had been boring.

"What is it?" Max asked, those unique amber eyes focused on her. Today they seemed rimmed in a rich brown. As usual with Max, he was attuned to her mood changes and thoughts, even if he wasn't aware what those thoughts were.

She glanced down. "My own laughter took me by surprise."

Max's brows furrowed. "Go on."

"I just realized it's been too long since I've laughed in my everyday life."

"Can we blame the asshole?" he asked, obviously trying to lighten the mood.

She shook her head, although she couldn't contain a smile. "I think the blame falls right here. I let my life get away from me. I let him control things and change the things about me and my life that made me happy."

"Have you asked yourself why?"

She didn't have to ask. She already knew. If she stayed with Lucas and let him mold her to fit his needs, she was in no danger of falling hard for him. No danger of becoming so emotionally attached that it would hurt when he left.

Was she ready to share something like that with Max, a man who accepted her as is and who she could fall for way too easily?

She blew out a deep breath. "I have, and it's complicated."

He reached out and brushed her hair behind her ear. "Well, we wouldn't want complicated to mess with the here and now."

"That's it? You aren't going to push for an explanation?"

"Nope. I'm going to do something else instead." His golden eyes glittered with determination and more than a hint of desire.

"What might that be?" she asked, leaning in. The closer she got to him, the more she could inhale the masculine scent that drove her crazy.

"I'm going to make sure you focus on having fun now and every day we're here. I don't want you to forget what it feels like to live life. And enjoy."

Her heart beat faster at the prospect, because it had been so long since she'd done just that, and Max seemed to understand.

"Where do we start?" she asked.

"With fantasies. Nothing more fun than some fantasy play, right?" he asked with a sexy wink.

"Umm, right?" She ran her tongue over her dry lips. "When you say play, do you mean the kind of play you did at Paradis?" she asked, naming the sex club he belonged to.

His jaw tightened at the question. "What do you know about the club?"

She swallowed hard. "Just that you, Decklan, and Amanda have gone there. And there was one in LA."

He narrowed his gaze, the dangerous look in his eyes setting her nerves on edge. "You've been there?" he asked incredulously.

She shook her head. But she'd wanted to check the place out. At the very least, she was drawn to the idea of being dominated.

Max blew out a long breath. "But you were curious."

Again, she nodded.

"About which part?"

She tilted her chin and met his gaze. "I find the idea of being dominated . . . exciting. Which makes sense, I guess, considering I let Lucas basically run my life."

"No. That's not the same thing. What Lucas did was selfish. Dominance and submission . . . it's a gift." He stared at her for a long while, assessing her and clearly thinking.

She didn't know what was going on in his head, and she twisted her hands nervously in her lap.

"Stand up."

"What?" She blinked at the demanding tone in his voice.

"I said, stand up."

Same commanding voice, and Lucy rose without thinking.

A slow, sexy grin edged his lips. He folded his arms across his tanned chest, his muscles a thing of beauty. He lounged even more casually against the sofa, his relaxed position at odds with the note of power in his tone. It didn't escape her notice that she responded to that command. Her breasts felt full, her nipples tight and pressing against the flimsy white dress, something he had to have noticed.

"Remove your dress," he said.

"What?" She glanced at him, startled. But her pulse began to pound, and arousal seeped from her sex.

"You heard me, princess. Undress."

She shook her head, about to balk . . . when understanding dawned. He was showing her what the sex club was like. What being dominated was like. He was inviting her into this part of his world. And offering her a way to find herself again, to let go and enjoy.

"I'm waiting." He drummed his fingers against the cushion, his impatience showing.

She stood at a crossroads. She could say no, and he'd snap back to the easygoing Max she normally dealt with, or she could . . . *play*.

Lucy gathered every Dare family trait she possessed—strength, courage, and fortitude—and made the decision to indulge and enjoy. She reached down, grabbed the hem of her dress, and pulled it over her head, tossing it onto the floor beside her, then faced the man of her dreams.

Max stared at the vision before him and wondered what he'd done to get so fucking lucky. It'd been a gamble, pulling his dom voice on Lucy, but everything inside him said to pull her in and keep her close. She wanted this. And he was determined not just to keep her enjoying life but to show her the difference between some asshole boyfriend telling her what to wear and how to style her hair and the beauty in what they could be to each other.

And beauty was such a mild word for what he saw when he looked at her. He rose to his feet and walked around her, taking her in. The long, lustrous dark hair hanging down her back; the nicely rounded breasts and rose-colored areoles; tight, perky nipples.

"You. Are. Perfect." His gaze traveled downward to the bare mound he'd felt earlier.

She visibly shivered. "I don't make it a habit to walk around the house naked. Or to stand at attention while some guy studies every inch of me."

He stepped into her personal space and tipped her chin so she met his gaze. "As to the first, if you lived with me, you damn sure would walk around the house naked."

Her eyes opened wide, her thick lashes blinking in surprise.

"And as far as the second, I'm not just some guy." He leaned in and nipped at her lower lip. "I'm your guy. For now," he quickly added before she could put up any mental or emotional barriers. "And your guy is going to make you feel good. Let's sit."

He picked her up and settled them back on the couch, her naked skin warm and sexy as she curled into him. He stroked his hands along her back and hip, seducing her with his touch until her body gradually relaxed in a way that told him she was finally getting comfortable with the whole naked thing, which was exactly where he needed her to be.

"So about making me feel good . . ." She glanced up at him, a little shy and a whole lot curious. "What do you have in mind?"

"Well, first I thought we'd have more to eat," he said, doing his best to ignore the fact that he was hard as a rock, and she would feel the evidence soon enough. The denim on his jeans was soft when he'd pulled them on, but now it chafed against his swelling cock.

He ignored the discomfort and looked over at the selection of food on the table. Bypassing the real meal, his eyes went directly to dessert. He took the top off of the Nutella sauce that came with the zeppole he'd ordered and slid his finger through the creamy sauce.

"Ooh, a man who goes right for sweets. Be still, my heart." She placed a hand over his chest instead of her own and sighed dramatically.

He grinned and smeared the treat onto her lower lip, then set about licking her clean, his tongue sliding over and around her mouth before heading inside so she could have a taste. His tongue stroked hers back and forth, deliberately keeping things light.

"Oh, yummy," she murmured against his mouth.

"My kiss or the Nutella?"

"The Nutella, of course." She grinned, and his heart beat faster in his chest at the sight.

He had her relaxed and comfortable. Time to up the ante. He grasped her hair and tugged her head back until her gaze met his.

She gasped at the unexpected pull. "Max!"

"Got a problem, princess?" He tugged harder, then sealed his lips over hers, changing the kiss from fun and playful to hard and demanding, controlling her position with his hands in her hair, keeping her neck bent so he could devour her mouth. And she let him, moaning as he staked his claim.

He slid a hand down her neck to her chest, until he reached her nipple and pinched hard. She moaned, squirming against him, clearly enjoying harder play. He knew he did, and watching her fall into the sensations he was giving did something for him, made him feel powerful and so fucking hungry for her.

Lucy's lips were bruised from Max's possessive kiss, her nipples aching from his touch, and her entire body was on fire, every nerve ending centered on her pussy. Her sex throbbed; her core felt empty and needy. But Max didn't seem in any rush to get to the main event.

He dipped his finger into the Nutella and rubbed it over her nipple, the cool sensation a shock to her tender flesh. He bent his head and licked up the creamy spread, his warm breath another stark, contrasting sensation that sent a heated thrill through her.

She couldn't focus worth a damn, was unable to lift her hands to touch him or reciprocate anywhere, not that he seemed to want it. No, his sole focus was her pleasure and the occasional delicious bite of pain. She'd never experienced anything like it, and he was taking her to sensual places she'd never been before.

Meanwhile, he continued to play, coating her belly button and the trail down to her sex with a dessert she'd never think of the same way again. He set her back on the couch and proceeded to lick it up, his tongue trailing over her skin, her belly undulating of its own accord. With each lap, her sex pulsed hard, and desire flashed through her brain. She needed his tongue lower against her clit, making her come, and she tangled her fingers tightly in his hair and pushed his head in an attempt to move things along.

He rewarded her with a nip of his teeth and lifted his head to meet her gaze. There was a bit of Nutella in the corner of his mouth, but before she could call attention to it, he licked it away. And her mouth watered at the sight, her entire body quivering with need.

"You're a bad girl, princess. I told you that I'm calling the shots." He rose to a standing position, keeping her in his arms, and strode to his bedroom, dumping her on the center of the bed.

He stood over her, a bare-chested god she wanted to crawl on top of and fuck until she screamed her release. There it was. He'd ramped up her need, had gotten her to the point where all she craved was him. Hot, hard, and thrusting inside her. From the bulge she'd felt while sitting on his lap and the thick outline in his jeans, there was no doubt he had to want the same thing.

"Max, come here." She crooked a finger his way.

"Not so fast," he said in that überalpha tone she was coming to love, that made her wet and breathless. "First, I want to know how much you really want to play." He eased one hip down on the bed and slid next to her. He lifted her chin with his hand. "You have to know, your answer has nothing to do with how much I want you. You could say no, and I'd be perfectly happy with vanilla sex as long as it was with you."

"Vanilla?" she asked, confused by his term and aroused by the notion that he had even more in store for her.

"In the club world, vanilla refers to people who have regular sex with . . . no kink." He opened the drawer beside the bed and pulled out a pair of padded cuffs. "These are kinky." He winked while handing them to her to feel.

She swallowed hard, surprisingly turned on by the idea of being bound by him. She ran her hands over the padding on the inside. "You brought these with you?"

He shook his head. "I know more about your fantasy island than you think. Anything I wanted, they were willing to supply."

He handily hooked one end of the cuffs to the slatted headboard and held the other out to her. "Your choice."

She didn't have to think long or hard. Instead, she held out her hands. She wanted this with him. Needed it.

"You trust me," he said gruffly.

"I do."

His eyes softened, and the kiss he placed on her lips was gentle and giving. His mouth was warm, a combination of nuts and chocolate, and she could live on his taste.

He broke their connection too soon and stood beside the bed. "Arms over your head."

She obeyed immediately and felt the thick cuffs wrap around first one wrist, then the next, each closing with a definite click that echoed throughout her body. She tugged and found herself bound, a scary feeling that caused her to struggle against the cuffs.

"Relax." He placed a calming hand on her forehead. "You say the word, I'll release you immediately."

"A safe word?" she asked.

"I think *no* will work for us. Red if you really want one." He stared into her eyes. "Are you good?"

She looked at him and grinned. "Green. Sir."

His golden-brown eyes darkened, and his hands went to the waistband of his jeans. In seconds, he'd shed them. Apparently he hadn't felt the need for boxers or briefs, giving her a first glimpse at his gorgeous cock. Her hands itched to wrap around his thickness and just feel.

Of course she couldn't move, could only look, her desire amped up at the sight. He placed one knee on the bed, then the other. He pulled her legs apart and settled between them.

"What are you thinking?" he asked.

She hesitated because she'd never expressed her desires out loud. Okay, she'd rarely had these kinds of desires before Max. Never had them was more like it.

"You're going to have to tell me if you want anything more to happen tonight." He held his cock in his hand and rubbed the engorged length over her sex, back and forth, coating himself in her wetness, teasing her with strokes of heat and hardness that felt good but were not enough to take her over that edge he'd built her up to. And kept her at now.

"I want to . . . taste you."

He leaned over, making sure to align their bodies, his erection in direct contact with her clit, and pressed a scorching-hot kiss on her lips. He thrust his tongue in and out, groaning as he mimicked sex by fucking her mouth.

Ripples of pleasure, like mini fireworks, went off everywhere, and she began to rotate her hips in an attempt to generate the friction she needed to come.

He lifted his head and grinned. "How was that? For a taste?"

She narrowed her gaze. "Not quite what I had in mind."

He shrugged, rolling one shoulder. "Then you're going to have to be more specific."

Lucy sighed and forced out the unfamiliar words. "I want to taste your cock." And while she was at it, she decided she might as well lay it all out there. "And then I want you to fuck me. Hard." Because she was so empty and needy she *hurt*.

A satisfied smile lifted his lips. "That wasn't so difficult, was it?"

"It wasn't easy," she said with a pout.

"But I'm going to make it worth your while." He edged closer until he hovered over her, pausing with his cock between her breasts.

His gaze never leaving hers, he pushed the twin mounds closer until she cradled his erection, and he began to thrust back and forth, sliding his hard cock through her softer flesh, and she moaned at the erotic feel.

"No." His sharp tone and a pinch on her nipples brought her out of the haze of desire she'd been lost in. "No way will I come on you when all I've ever dreamed of is coming inside you." He pumped his hips back and forth once more before moving up until his cock was within tasting distance . . . so she did.

He was salty and warm, and she opened her mouth wider. He slid his cock inside slowly, almost reverently, afraid to hurt her or choke her. Emboldened by their play and by her trust in Max, she slid her tongue along the velvety ridges before pursing her lips around him and doing her best to arouse him with her limited movement.

He pumped his hips once, twice, all the while maintaining perfect control before pulling out with a low groan. "You keep amazing me," he said as he reached over and pulled condoms from the nightstand drawer.

"You really do have whatever you need here. Should I worry you thought I was easy?" she asked, teasing.

He ran a hand through his already-tousled hair. She wanted to touch that, too, and pulled on the cuffs. "Had enough?"

"I just want to touch you too," she said, feeling vulnerable at the admission.

His eyes softened, and in seconds, he released her from the bindings. He rubbed her wrists between his palms. "Just want to make sure your circulation is okay and there are no bruises." He lifted each hand up for examination. "Just a little redness, something to remind you of this moment," he said, sounding pleased.

She had a hunch she would be satisfied, too, if she saw marks of his possession. Not too many or too hard. Just enough to remind her that she'd been his to command.

"One day I'll fuck you that way. But this first time? I'm going to make love to you, and I want you one hundred percent engaged."

The words *make love* shocked her, resonating in her brain and scaring her in so many ways. Brushing off her fears, assuring herself the words were just that, she pushed them away. Meanwhile, he grabbed the condom, ripped it open, and rolled it on.

Then he was back, his hands on either side of her head. He looked into her eyes, and every dream she'd had and pushed away came true. Before she could think, he was positioned at her core, thrusting hard, and she couldn't think at all.

Jaw tight, he glided out of her slowly before penetrating her harder and deeper than before. She moaned and bent her knees, wanting him in as far as he could possibly go, their bodies joined completely. He braced his hands on her knees and pushed her legs back, opening her to him completely.

"God, Max."

"Want to see you and feel you, princess." He pulled out and watched as he took her again. And again. And again.

She slid her fingers through his hair, doing a little pulling of her own as she worked her way down, using her freedom to touch. She felt every corded muscle in his shoulders, forearms, and back, scoring his skin with her nails as he pounded into her, grinding his hips with every thrust. She gasped at the sensation of him thick inside her, her own slick lubrication guiding him in and out.

She was lost in sensation, lost in Max, when suddenly he gripped her knees harder, and she knew he was close. That knowledge spurred her higher, sensations hitting her from inside and out, her orgasm exploding throughout her body.

She heard herself cry out as she bucked beneath him.

"Fuck. Lucy!" he shouted, his climax consuming him at almost the same time.

He slammed into her one last time, hitting a spot inside her she'd never known she had. Another orgasm immediately took hold, and she rolled her hips, grinding her clit hard against him until the sensations subsided.

She fell back against the mattress, damp with sweat. Max rolled off her but remained close, an arm wrapped around her as they both struggled for breath.

"Fucking amazing, princess." He kissed her forehead and pushed himself up and out of bed. "Be right back."

As he went to take care of the condom, Lucy's heart rate sped up in her chest, and she didn't think it would be returning to normal any time soon, because Max had utterly consumed and devastated her, mind, body, and soul.

Chapter Five

*B*efore Lucy knew it, the day of the wedding arrived.

Eden would have been an amazing place for prewedding festivities . . . if the bride had been healthy. Unfortunately Amanda still wasn't, and the prewedding activities originally scheduled for after Gabe and Isabelle arrived were canceled. No rehearsal dinner, no spa day for the women. Lucy felt awful that the bride-to-be had to miss out on so much. When she asked Decklan if she could visit with Amanda, he said she was spending most of her days throwing up and needed to conserve her energy for the wedding—which she insisted would go on as planned, no matter how sick she happened to be.

So Lucy had had the extra time to spend with Max. For the last forty-eight hours, she'd felt as if the outside world didn't exist. She'd lived in a haze of passion, sex, sun, and a happiness that was foreign to her, making her realize she'd merely been going through the motions of life. Any time nervous thoughts about the future or getting too attached to him intruded, they disappeared as quickly as they'd come. Almost as if the island didn't want her to deal with her hang-ups and insecurities while she was here. Considering the island was known for giving people their wildest dreams and fondest wishes, she didn't need to question things with Max beyond that.

She decided to go with the flow and enjoy her first experience with hot, fantastic sex. Sex that taught her about trust and communication and mutual satisfaction, all things that had been missing in her previous encounters. Max set the bar so high, she might never feel this kind of desire again, let alone have a truly passionate encounter with another man.

Shaking that thought off, she pulled the dress for the wedding out of her closet and laid it on the bed. Max had gone for a walk on the beach, but Lucy needed extra time to prepare for the big event. She'd showered in the luxurious bathroom with more jets than she knew what to do with . . . although Max had had some extremely creative ideas, and she'd come more than once thanks to his talented hands and the pulsing spray. Just another way Max had spoiled her for other men, other showers, and a future without him.

She slid her silk robe off her shoulders, leaving herself in a barely there thong that wouldn't show beneath her dress and a strapless lace bra. Lost in thought, she was startled when Max came up behind her.

He braced his hands on her shoulders, swept her hair out of the way, and placed an openmouthed kiss in the crook of her neck. His lips were warm, his breath hot, his tongue gliding sensuously across her skin. She shivered at the seductive touch, especially when he slid his hands down her shoulders, over her arms, and then cupped her breasts, squeezing hard on her nipples.

She moaned and leaned back into him, feeling his hard cock against her ass. "We have to be at the main hotel in thirty minutes, fully dressed. We don't have time for me to shower again and redo my hair."

But instead of stepping away from him, she wriggled further against him, inflaming her desire until moisture coated her thong. He slid his hand down her belly toward her pussy, and she stopped caring about their being late. She leaned her head back and spread her thighs.

"You like being a dirty girl for me, right?" Over the course of the last two days, Max had gotten increasingly more verbal during sex, encouraging her with hot, erotic words. "I asked you a question," he said with a pinch on her clit.

"Ouch! Oh," she said, moaning as the pain blossomed into something hotter and somehow infinitely sweeter. "Yes, yes, I like being a dirty girl."

He held her in place with a hand around her neck, hard enough for her to feel his command, gentle enough not to leave marks or cut off her breath or hurt her in any way. As she'd come to expect, his dominance turned her on even more. She liked when he held her in place and directed their play.

He skimmed her clit back and forth, occasionally squeezing the sensitive nub between his thumb and forefinger, driving her mad with need. She worked her hips back and forth, grinding herself against his palm, but he refused to allow her relief. Between her sore nipples and the exquisite pulsing need soaking her sex, she was ready to turn around and climb him right here and now. But she knew that wouldn't accomplish what she wanted. He'd drag this on longer, keeping her on edge.

Suddenly he nudged her forward, easing her upper body onto the mattress, and, without warning, smacked her ass with his hand. The first time he'd tried it, she'd been shocked, horrified, and thought she might cry. And then he'd smacked her other cheek. And suddenly the pain had morphed into pleasure, and she'd found herself rising in time to meet his hand.

"Do you know how fucking hard you get me? Seeing my handprint on your ass? Knowing you want my cock deep inside your wet pussy?"

He smacked her ass cheek again, and she began to grind her sex against the mattress.

"No. Only I can make you come. Now hold still."

She did as he commanded and was rewarded with the sound of a condom wrapper. Relief was imminent, she thought, and she imagined him sliding the latex over his thick, straining erection. Then he'd shove himself inside her, fast and hard.

She whimpered at the thought of him actually doing what she imagined.

He kicked open her legs, first one, then the other, positioning her, one hand on her lower back. And then his cock was poised at her entrance.

"Tell me what you want, princess." He smoothed his calloused palm over her tender backside, gently caressing her skin.

"You, Max. I want you."

"And I want you. So much." With a groan, he gave her what she asked for, thrusting deep inside.

So deep, she felt him everywhere. Her body had been his from the moment he'd taken her the first time, and she responded to him immediately now. She pulled at the comforter, curling her fingers into the material for support as he pounded into her. It was fast, it was a quick fuck, and yet it was no less meaningful for not being face-to-face.

Suddenly Max hit her G-spot, and her orgasm took over almost instantly. She flew apart, her heart soaring along with her body.

And as she came back to herself afterward, she'd learned that intimacy took many forms, but every time with Max was better and more special than the last. Every time with Max was a form of making love. And keeping her heart intact until she returned to New York was going to be much harder than she'd thought, if not damned near impossible.

He rolled to the side, flipping her onto her back and looking into her eyes, his expression full of concern. "Did I hurt you?"

She blinked back tears of emotion, a combination of ecstasy and fear still bouncing around inside her. "No."

A smile lifted his lips. "I had a hunch we'd be fucking awesome in bed."

She rolled her eyes. "You're lucky I find that confidence of yours charming and not annoying."

"As long as you'll take me," he said, rubbing his nose affectionately against hers.

The gentle gesture, so at odds with the dominant man who'd pounded her into the mattress, helped him tunnel even deeper into her heart.

She shoved at his shoulder, eager to get up and put space between them. "We need to get dressed." She rose to her feet, realizing she was sore and she needed a quick shower. Again. Somehow she'd have to keep her makeup intact, because she didn't have time to redo everything.

He rolled over onto his back and laid one hand over his head. "I can't believe Decklan's getting married. But man, from the minute he laid eyes on Amanda, he knew she was the one. No matter how hard he fought it," Max said.

Lucy swallowed hard. "They're perfect for each other," she managed to say to Max before walking into the bathroom and shutting the door.

As she turned on the water and waited for it to heat up, her thoughts wandered from Max to her brothers. Both subjects unsettled her. She'd tried very hard not to dwell on the fact that in a couple of hours, both Gabe and now Decklan would be married. The brothers who had raised her, been there for her, taken care of her after their parents had died were moving on with their lives. Wedding vows meant that someone else now came first.

Not Lucy.

It was normal. It was the way things should be. Them being happy and settled reminded her that she . . . wasn't. It was time to correct that. She needed to find a way to have a happy life without risking her fragile heart and even more fragile emotions.

Because Decklan's marriage signaled it was time to move back to New York and do as Isabelle said. She could watch Noah, and any other children her brothers had, grow up. She could enjoy a successful career and her family. Tomorrow morning she would fly back to New York with the memories of Max to keep her warm. It was more than she'd had before. And if she didn't want to suffer true loss again, she had to be satisfied with that. Satisfied with what she and Max had shared, and begin the painful process of pulling away again, now.

By the time Max and Lucy cleaned themselves up—separately, since she'd locked the bathroom door for her shower—her happy mask was back in place. The one Max hadn't seen since she'd given in to enjoying their time together on Eden. Something had flipped a switch in her brain, and she'd erected both physical and emotional barriers that had been missing for the last couple of days.

He couldn't say for sure what was going on in that beautiful head of hers, but he had a hunch that it had everything to do with the wedding bells that were about to ring. He was also sure Lucy thought he'd allow her to get away with her aloof behavior because he wouldn't start trouble in front of her family.

She'd be wrong. He had every intention of pushing his boundaries and hers.

They took the golf cart back up to the main resort, Max very much aware of Lucy sitting beside him. Dressed in a short coral strapless dress with a bandeau top, she was the epitome of island sexy down to her flip-flops that she'd remove in favor of bare feet when they walked to down to the beach for the ceremony. Her floral scent was spicy and arousing, reminding him of every moment he'd spent inside her and getting to know her, inside and out.

They approached the castle, which, frankly, he thought looked haunted, and the cart driver let them out. They walked up steps that were built into the mountainside. He left her alone with her thoughts, knowing not much would change now. He was biding his time, relying on the only strategy he had. The support of her family for them as a couple.

No sooner had they stepped into the main hotel than a woman met them in the lobby, as if their entrance was clocked and recorded. She directed them to the terrace room, where the wedding was being held, and he walked beside Lucy to the big, open double doors. Right before stepping inside, he laced his fingers through hers, determined to make a statement to this stubborn woman in front of her brothers.

Lucy immediately tried to jerk her hand away, but Max held on tightly and pulled her into the room.

"Lucy!" Gabe called as he made his way across the room toward her, his son in his arms.

She tried one last time to free herself. Max shook his head, though she wasn't looking at him, and merely curled his hand tighter around hers.

She turned and glared before her brother reached them. "Hi!" she said to her sibling before she turned her focus to the little boy in his arms. "And hi there, little man. How are you, Noah?"

"Dah." He held a chubby hand out to her, and Max was forced, then, to relinquish his grip.

It was his pleasure, because he got to see Lucy's face soften as she lifted her nephew into her arms and settled him on one hip. "Just look at you, so handsome in your tuxedo, like your daddy."

"Dah dah," he said this time, placing a hand on Lucy's chest. She giggled, the sound light and musical to Max's ears. "No, I'm Aunt Lucy."

"Dah."

"That's my smart boy," Gabe said, beaming.

Max envied him that happiness. The kind he'd never found in his marriage. The familiar pang of guilt he'd learned to accept and live with hit him when he thought of Cindy, but it quickly washed away on the sound of Lucy's laughter. He'd been young, too wrapped up in his parents' failings and in the past. He'd learned and come to terms. He'd even gone to Cindy's grave and made his peace there, as best he could.

Now his focus had to be on the woman who was living wrapped in the same pain of the past as he'd once been. He'd brought himself out in one piece, and he was determined to do the same with her.

"How was your vacation?" Lucy asked her brother. "I know this place has special meaning for you."

Gabe and Isabelle had cemented their love here and discovered she was pregnant with Noah here as well.

"Let's just say bringing along a babysitter was the right move," he said with a grin on his face that Max took to mean he'd had quality time alone with his wife.

"And we can change the subject," Lucy said, laughing. "I don't need to envision you and Isabelle . . . you know." She shook her head at her brother.

"Everyone's here!" Isabelle's happy voice interrupted whatever might have been said next. She approached, wearing a dress in the same color and similar style to Lucy's. Isabelle's figure was lusher and curvier, and each dress accommodated the individual woman's assets.

Everyone said their hellos, hugs were exchanged, and baby Noah toppled himself into his mother's waiting arms.

"So how was *your* vacation?" Gabe asked, not missing a beat from their earlier conversation and turning the tables with his question.

"Great. Relaxing," Lucy said, not meeting anyone's gaze.

Max raised an amused eyebrow and took this as his cue. He stepped close to Lucy, wrapped an arm around her waist, and pulled her close. "We've had an amazing time. Did you know you could rent private cabins on the beach?"

"No, I didn't!" Isabelle said, her astute gaze traveling back and forth between Max and a now squirming Lucy. "How romantic!"

"And now it's my turn to change the subject," Gabe muttered. "Although I will say it's about time." He slapped Max on the shoulder, his hand clamping down hard, a renewed reminder and warning to treat his sister right.

"Gabe!" Lucy chided, obviously horrified her brother was getting in the middle of her love life.

"What? We all know you two were just a matter of time," Gabe said.

"I—Umm—"

"We're going to take a walk." Max grasped Lucy's hand and led her out to the terrace, which overlooked the beach and ocean.

He walked her over to a chair and, with a gentle push on her shoulders, settled her in. He braced his hands on the arms and bent to face her. "What's going on? Are you embarrassed we're together?"

She frowned up at him. "We're not together, Max. We're having a vacation fling."

"So I'm right," he said, his gaze narrowing. "You've been on edge and pulling away."

She stiffened and looked away. "I don't know what you mean."

The hell she didn't. He gripped her chin in his hand and forced her to face him, ignoring the annoyed look in her eyes.

"You locked me out of the bathroom while you showered," he said, frustration filling him at the memory.

"So we wouldn't get carried away again and be late!"

Irritation bit at her tone, but he wasn't buying it and raised an eyebrow at the blatant lie. "You tried to pull your hand away before we walked in here. And you tried to downplay what really happened between us on the island."

"Because my brothers don't need their little sister's sex life thrown in their face!"

"And you're pulling away now. What happened to the woman who promised to chill and enjoy what the island brings?" Max asked, using her own words to call her out.

Lucy cringed, knowing he was right. "I—" *I didn't want to suffer any more loss,* Lucy thought, but she didn't want to admit that out loud.

The intensity that had been building between herself and Max on the island scared her, as did what this wedding symbolized in her life. More than anything, Lucy needed to get back to New York and begin building a life there. Alone.

"Decklan and Amanda are ready!" Isabelle called out, interrupting them from further conversation.

Lucy blew out a long breath, knowing she'd been given a reprieve. "We need to get going," she said, rising from her seat and smoothing the wrinkles in her dress.

Max frowned and stood up too. "This isn't finished," he warned her. "I have a lot I want to say to you."

Lucy didn't reply, because they didn't have time for an argument, and Max knew it too. She turned to face him. She stared into his handsome face, memorizing his features. Although they'd be working together in New York, things would never be the same between them again.

"Thank you for this time here," she said to him. "It was really wonderful."

He narrowed his gaze. "Why does that sound like good-bye?"

Before she could answer, they were joined on the terrace by Gabe, Isabelle, and a very dapper-looking Noah in his daddy's arms. Lucy grinned at the sight.

Decklan walked outside next. "We're supposed to go down to the beach. Amanda will meet us there," he said, shifting from foot to foot.

"Nervous?" Gabe asked, slapping his brother on the back.

"Nah. I just want this over with so I can call her my wife."

Lucy's heart did a sweet yet painful thump in her chest.

A little while later, they stood beneath a white canopy surrounded by island flowers. A light ocean breeze blew gently, bringing with it the salty smell of the ocean and sound of the waves lapping at the shore.

Amanda walked down the aisle in a white, flowing dress, gliding toward her waiting groom. Decklan waited with a big grin on his face, his eyes on his future wife. Lucy was happy for her brother, but that tender lump in her throat and catch in her chest remained throughout the ceremony.

Still, it was a happy occasion. The bride and groom kissed . . . long and intimately, making Lucy squirm, and her gaze fell on Max, his amber eyes watching her solemnly. He was concerned about the change in her mood, and she silently acknowledged he had every right to worry.

Although she planned to celebrate, dance, and enjoy the postwedding party along with her family, she'd also called ahead and secured a room in the castle for the night, along with the first flight off Eden in the morning. Max wouldn't be happy, but he wouldn't start an argument in front of her family either.

She was counting on it.

Chapter Six

*M*ax had been back in New York for three weeks, and time hadn't cured his hurt, anger, or frustration with Lucy. She'd not only left him alone their last night in Eden, opting to stay at the castle—with no real excuse for not returning to their cabin—but she'd taken the first flight out, leaving him to travel back to New York alone. No notice, no warning. Only the fact that he understood her panic and the reasons behind her fear enabled him to back off.

Insanity begged him to dominate her in real life the way he had in bed. Tie her up and keep her under his control until she believed they were meant to be. Thank God he was saner than that, but the need to see her didn't abate. Memories of their time together assaulted him constantly, along with the desire to bury himself in her sweet body and never leave.

He wished fixing her issues were as simple as holding her in his arms and vowing he'd never abandon her, but life wouldn't let him make those kinds of promises. Shit happened, as they both knew too well. So instead of storming her defenses, he gave her space and time after Eden, opting instead for a slow, steady assault.

Step one, bringing them back together for a legitimate reason. He sat in the empty shell of the restaurant he planned to open and glanced around at the old equipment from the original owners. Even that needed to be replaced with more modern pieces. He was ready to sit down with his chef and new designer and hammer out ideas.

He picked up his cell, pulled up Lucy's number, and hit send, wondering if she'd see his name flash on the screen and avoid the call. To his surprise, she answered on the first ring.

"Hi, Max," she said, her tone cautious but oh so welcome.

"Hi yourself, princess." He might be calling for business, but he'd be damned if he'd hide his feelings for her, and using his pet name for her came naturally.

"What can I do for you?" she asked in a formal voice.

He set his jaw, annoyed at the distance she was keeping between them. "I'm calling to set up a meeting between you, Sebastian Del Toro, and myself. I'd like you to see the space and get to work on ideas. That is, if you're still interested."

He held his breath.

"Yes. I definitely am. When did you want to meet?"

"I'll talk to Sebastian and get back to you."

"Great. In the meantime, I'll have a contract drawn up and sent over," she said, all business. "Oh! That's my other line. I look forward to hearing from you," she said and disconnected the call.

Max stared at the phone in his hand. She was taking playing hard to get to an extreme. Time to step up his game.

Lucy pulled together the contract her lawyer had drawn up for Savage Associates and Dare Designs. She grabbed her files, stuffed them in her briefcase, and headed downtown. She called for a car service early, leaving time for Midtown traffic, but the streets were empty, and she arrived early for their appointment.

She'd tried hard not to dwell on seeing Max, but of course, it'd been impossible. Max was on her mind, day and night. Her body missed his expert touch, the way he'd bring her to heights of ecstasy she'd never imagined existed and then hold her as they slept afterward. And she missed just talking to him during the day. In a short time, she'd come to enjoy his company, be it companionable silence or intense conversations.

And that was the part that enabled her not to go running back and apologizing for leaving him in Eden. It would be too easy to get permanently attached to the Max she'd come to know, not the man she'd thought she'd be having an affair with.

She'd convinced herself that they were on the same page when it came to not wanting a serious relationship. After all, he hadn't had a long-term girlfriend since his wife had passed away four years ago. But after their time together on Eden, she realized she'd underestimated what he needed and wanted from her. And even if she needed and wanted those same things, fear kept her from moving forward.

She arrived at the location in SoHo, impressed with the area immediately. They were within walking distance of NYU and right near a subway stop. As she approached the entrance, she paused to adjust the lapels on her suit, knowing a slight slip would reveal too much cleavage and send the wrong impression. But it was her favorite outfit, one she'd retired during her days with Lucas, and she needed all the armor she could get for today's meeting with Max.

She pulled on the restaurant door handle, surprised when it swung open. Because of potential vandalism, she'd thought it might be locked and she'd have to knock. Apparently she wasn't as early as she'd believed. Max must already be here, and her heart pounded harder inside her chest.

She stepped inside and was surprised by the stripped walls and floors. Apparently Max had already ripped out the prior interior designs. She took this to mean she'd have free reign over what went where, and the notion excited her artistic senses.

"Max?" she called out, her voice echoing in the empty space. "Is someone here?"

A good-looking man with jet-black hair stepped out from behind a set of double doors, and she immediately recognized him from television as Sebastian Del Toro.

"Hi. I'm here to meet Max Savage. I'm Lucy Dare, the designer."

The man came closer, and Lucy was struck by how handsome he was in a definite European way. "You must be Sebastian Del Toro," she said. "I've been looking forward to meeting you." She held out her hand.

"It's a pleasure, Ms. Dare." To her surprise, he lifted her hand and kissed it, holding on as he met her gaze.

"Call me Lucy, please."

"Once again, my pleasure. Max didn't tell me what a beautiful woman you are," he said in a sexy, deep voice. Despite knowing the man was a player, that husky voice made Lucy shiver.

"That's because her looks have nothing to do with her talent or ability to decorate a first-rate restaurant," Max bit out in a tone Lucy had never heard from him before. Not even with Lucas.

Max approached from what appeared to be the back of the restaurant, joining them and standing very close to Lucy. "I see you two have met."

"Yes, and this is going to be an even more pleasurable experience than I anticipated," Sebastian said.

"Let's get to work," Max muttered. "Over here." He led them to a bridge table and chairs that had obviously been set up as a makeshift workstation.

For the next hour, Lucy took notes on their vision and discussed her thoughts on color scheme and layout based on what she'd seen when she'd walked in the door. Knowing she needed a base of operations, she'd spent the last couple of weeks meeting with major design and construction firms in Manhattan and had agreed to freelance for one of the bigger ones. She needed a company that had architects and contractors ready to go and lawyers who could get building permits quickly.

She also needed an office and equipment, and the firm of Mann and Mann had been happy to lease her space and allow her to share a secretary with another part-time employee. If she was going to live in Manhattan, she needed to settle in quickly. And she had.

Turning her focus back to Max and Sebastian, she noted that she needed to have someone come in and take measurements, and she promised computerized 3-D renderings of her ideas as soon as possible.

While working, both Sebastian and Max dialed down the testosterone and focused on what was important, bringing the restaurant to life as soon as possible. The ideas flew among the three of them, and Lucy felt like she was part of a well-oiled team. Max was in his element, coolly and efficiently taking charge. Without realizing it, Sebastian was deferring to Max's vision, but as Max had pointed out, he still had the sense that he was in charge too.

Lucy studied the men as they talked, Max pointing at kitchen sketches that they were currently discussing. He was brilliant, and she enjoyed watching him work, engaged in something that excited him . . . *outside the bedroom*, she thought wryly, shifting in her seat. Because as soon as she thought of Max and the bedroom, her thoughts turned to sex.

She'd certainly spent enough time reliving their time on Eden. Inevitably she'd recall her hands being bound, her body at his mercy. The sensual heat of his thick erection as he thrust inside her and the hot slap of his palm against her ass. All those memories had her on edge, aroused, and doing the best she could to avoid writhing in her seat.

As if he could read her mind, he lifted his head and met her gaze, a knowing look in his amber eyes. And if her face hadn't already been heated, she was sure it was now.

"I think we've covered everything for today," Sebastian said.

Relieved and needing fresh air, Lucy nodded. "I agree, at least on my end." She gathered her files together and shoved them into her briefcase.

Max's phone rang, and he glanced at it. "Be right back. I need to take this." He stepped away to take the call, leaving her alone with Sebastian.

Sebastian turned to Lucy with a charming smile. "I'm looking forward to implementing your ideas. I think your idea of channeling the tapas bars in Barcelona is a smart one. An outdoor feel is exactly the right atmosphere."

"I agree."

"Let me walk you out," Sebastian said.

Lucy glanced back at Max, who seemed engrossed in a conversation that wasn't likely to end soon. As much as she wanted to stay . . . to spend more time with him, their business was finished for now, and the smarter thing would be to leave. She'd asked the driver to wait, so she could leave whenever she was ready.

She turned to Sebastian. "Okay . . . thank you."

He placed a hand on her back and led her to the door. His touch felt unfamiliar and wrong, and she stepped out of reach as soon as they were outside. The sun beat down overhead, and Lucy was happy to breathe in the fresh air and see sunshine. There was no air conditioning running inside, the lighting was dim, and the stuffiness had given her a headache.

Sebastian turned toward her, and she was struck by the aqua blue in his eyes. "I was wondering if we could meet up later and talk about ideas I had for the bar area? I didn't run them by Max yet. I wanted our designer's opinion first."

"Oh!" She didn't mind giving her professional point of view. "We could meet at Mann and Mann during the week," she suggested, not wanting to give him the wrong impression. He might be handsome and charming, but she wasn't interested in anything more than a professional working relationship.

"We could do that. Or . . . I'm meeting friends for drinks tonight at Glam," he said of the exclusive nightclub she'd been to before. "They're from different parts of the celebrity world. Maybe you'd like to meet them? If we can fit in some business, great; if not, we'll set up an appointment at your office."

Lucy grasped her briefcase tighter. This offer included a group of people—no worries about putting herself in an

awkward position with her newest client. And she was poten-
tially meeting new clients, she told herself.

"Why not? It sounds like fun." And fun wasn't something
she'd had much of since leaving Eden.

Sebastian smiled, showing the dimples that had won over
the world . . . or at least a great many females on TV while he
was cooking.

"Great. You gave me your card, so I'll text you later with the
place and time. Sound good?"

Lucy smiled. "It does. Thank you."

"I can't wait." He touched her back once more. "Is this your
car?" He gestured to the idling sedan.

She nodded, and he stepped closer, opening the back door
so she could climb inside.

"See you later, Lucy."

"Good-bye, Sebastian."

By the time Max hung up the phone with the manager of
another one of his restaurants who was having a problem with
staff, Lucy and Sebastian had disappeared.

Max cursed and stormed into the street in time to see a
black sedan pull away from the curb. Sebastian stood on the
sidewalk watching.

Max shoved him in the shoulder. "Stay the fuck away from
her."

Sebastian turned to stare Max down. "Do you have a say
in what she does? Because it didn't look like anything but
business to me."

Max narrowed his gaze. He had a hard enough time cor-
ralling Lucy. He didn't need the playboy chef adding to his
problems.

"Don't you have enough problems with Gia refusing to
accept that things are over?" Max asked of Sebastian's ex-
girlfriend. Stalker might be more like it, considering she had

a tendency to show up wherever Sebastian went and cause trouble.

"Gia's a lunatic. I should have seen it sooner."

"I'm not sure women come to you insane. I think you drive them to it." Because he couldn't keep his dick in his pants and didn't see anything wrong with cheating.

"She was freaking good in bed, buddy. I was blinded to her dark side."

Max rolled his eyes. His concern wasn't for Sebastian but for Lucy. Though he'd admit to jealousy, he was also looking out for her. She didn't need to get involved with a player like Sebastian. Problem was, she might see Sebastian as an easy-to-be-with alternative to Max and his intensity and the fact that he wanted more from her than an easy affair like she'd had with Lucas.

And that scared the crap out of him.

"Didn't anyone teach you that you don't shit where you sleep?" Max asked.

"Same could apply to you." Sebastian grinned, rolling his shoulder in a casual shrug at the same time.

Shit. "Then how about backing the fuck off because you have a little respect for your boss?"

Sebastian slapped Max on the back. "I'll think about it and get back to you."

And for the first time, Max regretted bringing Lucy in on his project.

After leaving SoHo, Max returned to his apartment and headed to the gym. He spent a long time beating the crap out of a punching bag, pretending it was Sebastian's pretty face instead. He had a soft spot for his old friend, and he appreciated his culinary talent, but the man was a cocky bastard with little respect for anyone else's territory. He winced, just imagining how Lucy would take him referring to her that way. He finished up with a sauna, then returned home.

He flipped his phone around in his hand, debating on acting on the urge to put an end to this nonsense and calling

Lucy. Time and space were well and good, but it wasn't helping him make headway with her. He needed to be with her again in order to convince her of what she was throwing away.

He dialed her number before he could change his mind. It rang and rang . . . He was about to hang up when he heard her voice, along with a lot of loud noise and music in the background. "Lucy?"

"Max!" Lucy said.

"Let me talk to him!" Max heard Sebastian's voice loudly beside her and gritted his teeth.

"Max, buddy. You should come party. It's awesome here!" Sebastian shouted into the phone.

"Where's here?" Max asked.

"Glam! I'll leave your name at the door."

"Sebastian, you'd better be watching out for Lucy until I get there," Max warned him.

"No worries. I'm taking good care of her," he said, laughing as he disconnected the call.

Max swore and headed to his bedroom to change into club-appropriate clothing or he wouldn't get into Glam, let alone near Lucy.

Lucy hadn't been out for fun since arriving in New York, and she arrived at Glam excited to finally have something to do in this city beyond brood over her love life. Sebastian had private seating, for which he'd paid more money than Elite normally collected for their best tables. The champagne was flowing to celebrate the fact that a guy named Darrin Coash had gotten an acting job and would be leaving for LA at the end of the week.

Sebastian hung with an eclectic group of celebrity types, men and women, Broadway and off-Broadway actors, soap opera stars, and wannabes who'd barely booked their first television commercial. All were fun and welcoming, and Lucy relaxed, sharing alcohol and listening to their stories.

She had a light, happy buzz going when her phone rang, and she saw Max's name flash on the screen. Instinct had her answering, pushing aside all those pesky concerns because she wanted to hear his voice.

"Max!"

"Let me talk to him!" Sebastian, who sat beside her, grabbed her cell. "Max, buddy. You should come party. It's awesome here!" He shouted to be heard over the background music and noise.

Max must have asked where they were, because Sebastian said, "Glam! I'll leave your name at the door." Then . . . "No worries. I'm taking good care of her," he said, laughing as he disconnected the call.

"Max is coming here?" she asked him.

"He sure is. Let the fun begin," Sebastian said, calling a cocktail waitress over and ordering another bottle of champagne.

She had another drink, then Sebastian grabbed her and led her onto the dance floor. With a fast beat going, they, along with everyone else, had their hands in the air, clapping and moving to the music. When the next song slowed things down, Lucy knew it was time to reclaim her seat.

Since it was too loud to speak, she pulled away from him and gestured to their table, set higher and behind a privacy rope. Sebastian shook his head, spun her, and pulled her against him, so she had no choice but to sway to the music.

Lucy decided to give in for this one dance, and then she'd leave without making a scene. To his credit, Sebastian didn't make a move. His hand remained on her lower back, never slipping to her ass, and he kept a respectful distance between them. The music ended, and it was silent for a few moments.

Sebastian lifted her hand and kissed her, bowing lightly. "Thanks for the dance, sweetheart."

Lucy was about to roll her eyes at his exaggerated gallantry when a brunette barged between them and shoved Lucy out of the way. "Get your hands off my man, you white trash bitch!"

Lucy stumbled back, hitting a hard male body. Strong hands grasped her shoulders, keeping her from falling. She righted herself and turned so she could apologize to the man, only to find it was Max who'd saved her from sprawling to the floor.

"What the fuck?" he asked over the music, which had restarted.

Lucy pointed to the brunette with the bad attitude, still screaming at Sebastian. A security guard had arrived and separated the two, but she was still spouting off and trying to get near him.

"That's his crazy ex," Max muttered.

She was crazy, all right. Lucy wasn't the type to get into a catfight with any woman, but she wasn't one to let someone walk all over her either. She started back toward Sebastian, but Max tugged her against him.

"Let Sebastian and security handle it," he said, keeping her close with an arm around her middle, sliding his hand around to her front, keeping his palm over her belly.

She liked this possessive side of him, which surprised her considering she'd spent her later teenage years dealing with overprotective men. But with Max's strong arms around her, the sense of comfort and familiarity turned more sexual, a reminder of how her body responded to him. Her nipples puckered, and her sex grew heavy and warm, an automatic reaction to his touch, and she sucked in a startled breath. How could a sane woman ever resist him?

"Sebastian, you okay?" Max asked, his voice rough in her ear.

Lucy blinked, coming out of her desire-filled stupor, and realized that one of the guards had, in fact, escorted the woman out of the club.

Sebastian, looking frazzled and less put together than he'd been earlier, met Max's gaze and nodded. "Yes." He shook his head as if clearing it, turning his attention to Lucy. "I'm sorry for that. I had no idea Gia was so damned possessive."

"That's not possessive—it's insane. I think you need a restraining order," Max muttered.

Lucy agreed with a nod.

"We'll see. I don't think she'll make such a public scene again. Getting thrown out of here is pretty damned humiliating on its own." His gaze fell to Max's hand, still on her stomach. "Speaking of possessive . . . what's going on between you two?"

"It's complicated," Lucy said.

"And none of your damned business, except you need to keep your hands off her from now on."

"Max!" Lucy said, embarrassed by his display. "Don't be rude!"

"Rude? Really? I walk in here and find you in his arms?" he asked as the music started up again. "I'll show you rude," he muttered and, without warning, hefted her over his shoulder and headed for the back hall.

Chapter Seven

"Max, put me down!" Lucy yelled at him, leaving him no choice but to aim a well-placed swat on her ass. He passed a few openmouthed people who said nothing as he strode past the restroom and into the back office.

"What the hell?" Mason Ford, the owner and a friend of Max's for years, jumped to his feet from behind the desk. "Savage, what's going on?"

"Put me down!" Lucy said, pounding on his back.

"Need your office for a little while," Max said, ignoring her.

Mason studied them warily. "Am I going to have the cops here later?"

"Yes!" Lucy said.

"No," Max promised him.

"Good enough for me," Mason said, striding past them. "Lock the door behind me, and call me when I can come back in." He turned back as he reached the entrance. "Good luck. Looks like you're going to need it." He chuckled and walked out, slamming the door behind him.

Max hit the lock before letting Lucy slide to her feet. "Max Savage, I could kill you. That was mortifying!"

"You want to talk about embarrassing? Did I or did I not find you in the arms of another man?" Every cell in his body rebelled against the notion. Hell, his pupils still burned from seeing Sebastian's hands on her back, her stomach, and her exposed skin.

"You and I aren't together!" Her blue eyes shot angry sparks.

"No?" he asked, his jaw aching from grinding his teeth together. "Okay, then you won't mind if I walk out there and pick up the first hot chick I find, take her home, and—"

Her hand shot out and covered his mouth. "Okay, you made your point!"

He couldn't stop the slow grin that spread on his lips but made sure to lick her palm before she yanked her hand away, sexual awareness finally back in her expression.

"That make you jealous, princess?" he asked, satisfaction filling him.

Because she couldn't deny it, she pouted instead. But Max wasn't finished making his point. Not by a long shot.

"Then how do you think I felt, calling you only to hear you were with Sebastian? Then walking in here and finding you wearing this sexy-as-fuck leather miniskirt and cropped top, with his hands all over you?" Max's blood boiled at the memory of what he'd seen.

She sighed, the defiant set of her shoulders slipping. "We were just dancing."

"His hands were on you," he bit out again. He grasped her thigh possessively in one hand, feeling the heat of her flesh against his palm. "Nobody has the right to touch this body except me."

"Max." The words came out on a husky whisper.

His hand drifted upward, barely teasing her damp panties. "Whose body is this?" he asked, his finger swiping teasingly over her covered clit.

She bit down on her lower lip and moaned, arcing her hips forward, seeking more contact.

"I mean it, princess. Answer me." He lifted her and settled her on the edge of the desk, shoving her skirt up and spreading her legs wide so he could step in between.

A glance down showed him her panties were, indeed, wet with desire. His cock swelled, the need to unzip and feel her hot pussy swell around him driving him hard.

But he was on a mission for more than a quick fuck she'd regret the minute it was over. When it came to Lucy, he was greedy. He wanted more. Hell, he wanted it all. He pressed his thumb hard against her swollen clit, unrelenting as he played with the hardened nub.

She moaned, her entire body vibrating with need. "I need to come," she managed, panting and arching her sex into his hand.

"And you will as soon as you tell me nobody else can touch this wet pussy except me."

He slid his finger beneath the scrap of fabric and rubbed hard over the distended bud, flesh to flesh this time, keeping his touch light enough to arouse. Not hard enough to allow for climax.

She leaned back, her breasts pressing insistently against her top, nipples poking out and begging him to suckle her through the fabric.

"Max, please." She drew out the last word, begging like he'd been dreaming of her doing.

"Is that *Max, I'm yours?*" His entire body was strung tight, and he hoped like hell she'd give in.

"You're still not playing fair," she groaned, every nerve ending electrified and in need.

"Haven't changed who I am," he reminded her, his voice gruff and dark with desire.

No, he hadn't.

And he wasn't saying anything her body didn't agree with. She already accepted that as long as Max was in the vicinity, she couldn't resist him. And why should she? They were going to be working together, spending time together . . . Why not sleep together? And when the project was finished, they would be too.

Then she could return to her way of safely picking men who couldn't capture her heart. She just needed to hold on to it during the time she and Max were together.

"What'll it be?" he asked in a harsh voice, accompanied by a rough flick to her clit that had stars flashing behind her eyelids and her body soaring toward climax.

"Fuck me, Max." She pulled at his shirt, yanking it from the waistband of his pants, then frantically unbuttoning them too.

"Then tell me what I want to hear." He grabbed her wrists and held them at her sides. "Who does this body belong to?" he gritted out.

"You."

"Say it."

"My body belongs to you."

"And?"

"My . . ." She ran her tongue over her lips and looked at him. His eyes were heavy-lidded, his gaze filled with desire. All for her. His entire being was focused on *her*, making it easier to give him the words he sought. "My pussy is yours too." The only thing she tried to hold on to was her heart.

Her stark words released his passion. He ripped off her underwear, shoving it into his pocket before stepping back to remove his pants and boxers. They hit the floor. Before she could think, he was back, his heavy cock pushing inside her.

She sucked in a breath as he worked his thickness into her, groaning as he plunged deep, filling her completely.

"Fuck, baby, you feel so good. I missed you."

Ignoring the lump in her throat and the emotions that came along with this moment, she leaned forward, breathing in his masculine scent and pressing her lips against his neck.

He groaned, his body quivering inside hers. "Lie back," he said in that commanding voice.

She did as he asked, ignoring the pens and papers digging into her upper back.

"Now bend your knees." She responded immediately. He grabbed her ankles and began to move, gliding in and out of her sex, sliding out, propelling himself deeper and harder on each thrust.

Her moans mingled with his, and she was forced to admit, if only to herself, that this felt amazing. So right. It wasn't just sex. With Max it was always so much more. He didn't just take charge of her body—he gave of himself as he drove her higher and closer to her climax. Her sex tightened, and sensation took over. Nothing mattered but him.

Having staked his claim, he forced her to face the truth. He dominated her. Possessed her. He owned her body, and she shattered, bringing her to heights she'd never experienced before. The kind she'd never know again.

They each took time to come back to themselves, and Lucy was glad. She needed a few minutes to process . . . although how you processed the mind-blowing sex that had wreaked havoc with your heart was beyond her.

Max rose and helped her to a sitting position. He found tissues, and they cleaned up in silence. Her heart beat rapidly inside her chest as she wondered what he expected from her now.

"We didn't use a condom."

His words were the last she'd expected. She should have thought about it, been smarter. They'd both been frantic and too aroused to think straight. Not that it was an excuse.

"I'm protected." She'd never wanted to worry about pregnancy with someone she wasn't planning on spending the rest of her life with. And since she never intended to have that kind of relationship, long-acting contraception seemed smart. Thinking about it now caused a sharp pain to lance through her chest.

"You're on the pill?" he asked.

"I have an IUD." She didn't meet his gaze, instead concentrating on fixing herself up for the walk back through the club. She shimmied her skirt down the best she could, well aware she didn't have any panties to put on underneath.

"Hey." Max tipped her chin up, forcing her to meet his gaze. "If anything happened, you wouldn't be in it alone. But since I know that's the last thing you want to talk about, we can move on. Pregnancy won't be an issue."

Exactly what she wanted to hear. So why did she feel suddenly sad? And blue? Bad enough her brothers and their marriages were stirring up uncomfortable feelings about their childhood and abandonment, but now Max was inadvertently tripping those emotions too.

She shivered, suddenly cold, and wished she had a sweater to put on over her shirt. As if sensing what she needed, Max pulled her into him, wrapping his arms around her tightly. "And you can trust me on everything else too. I haven't used the club in a while, but they insist on physicals, and I just had mine recently."

She swallowed hard. "Thank you. I was only with . . . Well, I made him use a condom."

She hadn't wanted that kind of connection with any man she slept with. In fact, Max had been the only man she'd ever slept with and forgotten to insist on that kind of protection.

"Ready?" he asked.

To go out and face the world after he'd carried her through the nightclub like a caveman? If not for the loud music outside these walls, she had no doubt everyone would have heard what they'd done in here . . . although once they got a look at her, they'd figure it out anyway.

"Might as well get it over with," she muttered, pushing herself away from him.

"We're not walking through the front entrance. We can go out the back. I have my driver waiting."

"You'll drop me off at my place?"

He studied her long and hard before answering. "No, Lucy. Either I'll come up and stay at your place, or you can pack and we'll go back to mine."

She blinked in shock. "Wait, what?"

"You agreed. Your body's mine, your pussy is mine. And if I want access to what's mine . . . we need to be together," he said as if he made all the sense in the world.

"Are you insane? I didn't agree to living with you!"

He folded his arms across his chest. "No, you didn't. If I had to guess at what's going on in that head of yours, it would go something like this. We can't keep our hands off each other; you want me as much as I want you. Since we're going to be working together, we might as well reap the benefits of sex too. Then when the restaurant is finished, we'll go our separate ways. How am I doing so far?"

She opened her mouth, closed it again, then forced herself to speak. "How did you figure all that out?"

"I told you once before, I know you."

"How?" She needed to know how he'd gotten into her head so easily.

"Because I *was* you once." He hooked his arm in hers and led her toward the door.

"Wait. Explain what you mean."

He paused, leaning one shoulder against the still-closed door. "I will. One day, when you're ready to really hear me, I'll explain everything." And on that cryptic note, he unlocked the door, placed a hand on her back, and led her to the waiting car.

Lucy stood in her bathroom, dressing to head out for a dinner with Max and Sebastian. But as she put the finishing touches on her makeup, her focus wasn't on their plans; it was on the sounds coming from the other side of the door. Max had installed a pull-up bar in the bedroom doorway for his workouts, and she heard him grunting on each exhale now.

The man was a sight to behold when he worked out, all tanned skin and muscles glistening with sweat, making her want to plaster herself to his sculpted body, inhale that masculine scent she associated with him, and never let go. She'd gotten used to him going through his daily routine. And wasn't that the kicker?

Never in her wildest dreams had Lucy thought Max was serious when he'd insisted that, one way or another, they were moving in together. Apparently he hadn't been kidding, because a month after that fateful night at Glam, they were sharing Gabe's old apartment. Of course, she could have told him he was crazy, said no, or done any other number of rational things. Instead, she'd looked him in the eye and called what she'd thought was his bluff.

"We can go back to my place," she'd said, too stunned by the fact that he had her all figured out. She was planning on walking away when the restaurant and their time working together was over. He clearly intended to make that as emotionally difficult for her as possible.

She assumed he'd get tired of not being in his own place a lot faster than she'd wear out her welcome at his. She'd been wrong. Thirty days, nights, and counting, and he seemed perfectly content with their new arrangement. And when he'd said he wanted access to her body for the time she'd allotted to them, he'd meant it.

He was a greedy lover. He woke her up with his hands on her body, moving leisurely over her flesh, kneading her breasts, or with his mouth on her sex. And she fell asleep at night exhausted from whatever kind of sex they'd shared, hot, fast, and hard . . . or slow and methodic lovemaking before he wrapped himself around her and passed out cold.

A girl could get used to his attentiveness in bed and out. And no doubt that was his intention as well. She'd been treated to breakfast in bed, to lunch brought to her at her new office space, to expensive dinners out, and to quick takeout pizza. Not to mention the home-cooked meals. Who knew the man had such talent in the kitchen? Although considering he owned restaurants, she should have realized he'd have culinary ability as well.

Savage in SoHo was moving forward at a rapid pace despite some initial glitches. Though Max and Sebastian had approved her designs, and she'd been able to order their furniture and décor with a six- to eight-week delivery time, there had been other delays. First had been the issues with the building permits for structural changes Max had filed early on. Somehow the paperwork had been lost, necessitating refiling. Red tape and bureaucracy were standard in Manhattan, and their start date had to be pushed back weeks. The date was still uncertain, as the permits had yet to be approved. Not even Mann and Mann's contacts had been able to push the paperwork through faster.

To add insult to injury, Sebastian had personal problems to deal with. His ex-girlfriend, Gia Lambert, had been making herself a general nuisance, showing up wherever Sebastian was and driving him insane. Apparently the woman didn't know how to accept *we're over*. Sebastian was supposed to be busy working on the menu, but he claimed Gia had disturbed his *artistic sensibilities*, and he couldn't concentrate. His lawyer was supposed to work on getting a restraining order ASAP, and in the meantime, they pushed forward with the plans.

Lucy had gone about organizing her life in New York. Mann and Mann had offered her an associate position, guaranteeing her clients and salary. Though she had family money, she prided herself on working for a living, even if her brother and the family business had provided that income thus far.

A quick knock on the bathroom door brought her out of her musings. "Come on in."

The door opened, and Max strode in, his upper torso glistening with sweat, the muscles in his chest and arms bulging and more prominent than ever thanks to his recent workout. She couldn't help but stare, sliding her tongue over her glossed lips in reaction.

"Like what you see, princess?"

"How can I not?" she asked honestly. He was cut on top, his waist trim, and those indentations right above his workout shorts were enough to make a girl go insane. "You need to shower, or we're going to be late," she said, her voice dropping to a husky level.

His golden eyes locked on hers. "Keep looking at me like that, and we won't make it out of here at all."

At the sound of his deep voice, her nipples hardened, and dampness coated her panties, almost as if on cue. "Max," she said, wanting the word to come out as a warning. Instead, it sounded more like a plea.

"Yes?" he asked, stepping closer.

He smelled of sweat and man, and her sex softened even more. "We have to go."

"Want to know what I'd do to you if we didn't?"

He walked forward, backing her against the vanity, close enough to tantalize and tease her senses but not enough to ruin her little black dress with his perspiration.

Though she shouldn't indulge the predator in him, she couldn't help wanting to know what he was thinking. "What would you do to me?" she asked, her imagination going wild at the thought of the varied scenarios her mind conjured.

"I'd spin you around," he said, doing just that until she was facing the mirror.

She gripped the cool granite counter with both hands and waited, her body strung tight.

"I'd lift this little dress up over your sweet ass."

In an instant, her butt was exposed to the cool air, courtesy of the barely there thong she'd chosen, and her breath deserted her in a rush.

A glance in the mirror showed her face was now flushed darker than the blush she'd applied.

"Then I'd bend you over the counter and rub my palm over your soft cheeks." Without warning, he pressed against her back, easing her upper body down and her ass up for his viewing pleasure.

He cupped one cheek in his hand, rubbing his calloused palm over her exposed flesh before squeezing so tight that she gasped at the first hint of delicious pain, immediately followed by the heated warmth of desire flowing through her veins. She dipped her head and let out a low moan, causing him to repeat the action on her other cheek.

"And then . . ." The words sounded raw and drawn from deep inside him. "Then I'd fuck you." He punctuated the words with a slap against her sensitive flesh.

"Oh!" She swallowed the word, her entire body vibrating with need.

"But it wouldn't be hard and fast," he said, following up with a strike on her other cheek that stung in the best possible way. "No, I'd take you slow and easy, so you felt every hard inch of my cock as I made you mine."

Lucy's mind had gone nearly blank, lost in a foggy haze of desire and need. Her sex pulsed, swelling with the need to be filled and used.

"Unfortunately, as you pointed out, we don't have time." He yanked her dress down, covering her sore behind and gently rubbing his hand over her now hidden ass.

"Max!" Groaning in disappointment and frustration, she spun around, only to glance down and find he was in no better shape than she was.

His thick erection tented his workout shorts, looking extremely uncomfortable behind the fabric.

"We can be late," she offered, no longer caring if they stood Sebastian up for dinner.

He shook his head, his jaw tight. "Wish we could, but he made reservations. You know how Sebastian is. He used his name and clout to get the best seat in the house. He wants to see and be seen."

"He wants people to bow and kiss his feet and tell him how they can't wait for his restaurant to open to the public. Got it," Lucy said, knowing Sebastian's cocky and slightly narcissistic side would be on full display.

"Right. And much as I'd rather skip it in favor of staying home with you, it'll be good publicity for us to be out with him."

She nodded in understanding. "But you didn't need to get me all worked up beforehand," she said, knowing full well she was pouting because he'd left her wanting. He hadn't even given her a good orgasm to hold her over.

"Yeah. I did. Because I wanted your mind on one thing only while we're out tonight."

"And what would that be?" she asked, although she already knew.

"Me."

The one consolation she had was that while she was thinking of all the naughty things he'd do to her later, when they got home, he'd be thinking about burying himself inside her too.

Turning away, she picked up a tube and swiped on some lip gloss, hoping she could fix her makeup so no one else knew she was sex-deprived and horny as hell.

Max had a damned hard time concentrating on dinner or Sebastian and their prime table when he was sporting a hard-on thanks to his earlier games in the bathroom. He wished he'd finished what he'd started. Instead, both he and Lucy were suffering. The flush heightening her cheeks and the way she squirmed in her seat told him that.

He turned his attention to his chef, who'd not only secured the table but chosen his seat facing out so he could meet and greet every famous person who walked by and some who weren't. Thanks to the man's stint on reality television and the fact that social media had turned him into a much-loved familiar face and name, most people were thrilled to shake Sebastian's hand and have a few words too. But every compliment went to his head, and his ego was big enough. Especially since the *chef* was having trouble creating the menu he'd sworn would come easily.

Blaming his ex-girlfriend wasn't cutting it anymore either. Sebastian needed to focus on business and not his celebrity status, a conversation Max planned to have with him once they got through tonight.

And since—despite her sexual frustration—Lucy seemed to be enjoying the evening, laughing and whispering her opinions on the tacky décor, Max decided not to worry about work for the time being. Instead, he marveled at the amazing fact that he'd been living with Lucy for the last month.

He hadn't *planned* on moving in with her. Hell, he'd spouted the words in a frantic attempt to keep her close, knowing that if she had her way, she'd sleep with him at night and keep him at a distance all day. He couldn't allow her to be in charge of their relationship that way. Once he'd suggested it, he sure as hell hadn't expected her to agree. But she had.

And it had taken a lot of work—pleasurable exertions, to be sure—for him to get her to a place where she'd relaxed and enjoyed them being together, and not just when they were in bed. It was the only way he could think of to bind her to him in ways that went beyond sex. Ways that she was inherently and desperately afraid of feeling. He definitely liked where they were now, but he wasn't fooled and knew they had challenges ahead.

She groaned at something Sebastian said, the sound bringing Max's focus back to the present.

"Oh shit," Sebastian suddenly muttered.

"What is it?" Max asked.

"Look who's here." The other man tipped his head toward a crowd of people, and Max caught sight of Sebastian's cooking show competitor, Anthony Abbadon, walking toward their table.

"Behave," Max said under his breath as Anthony reached them.

And if he thought Sebastian played star to the hilt, Anthony was a supreme diva. Where Sebastian wore khakis and loafers, Anthony was slicker, wearing a dark suit, white shirt, and tie, his blond hair smoothed back with gel.

"Sebastian, my friend, it's so good to see you!" Anthony walked over and slapped Sebastian on the back.

The two men traded pleasantries through gritted teeth. In public they were playing nice, but clearly there was no love lost.

According to Sebastian's account, Anthony resented how much the audience and social media loved Sebastian. And Sebastian had very much wanted to win the show, the money, and the job in New York. That he now would have his own kitchen and restaurant in SoHo didn't negate the sting of losing. He felt like he'd been humiliated in public by Anthony, who, rumor had it, had paid off one of the judges. Nobody could prove a thing. Which left the two men at odds, opening restaurants in the same city. The ultimate competition.

"And who is this lovely lady?" Anthony asked, his smarmy-eyed gaze zeroing in on Lucy.

Now Max's hackles rose.

"Lucy Dare," she said, extending her hand. "It's nice to meet you."

Anthony slid his hand over hers and held on. "Such a beautiful woman. You couldn't possibly be with Sebastian." He dropped the insult with a slick smile and enough sweetness toward Lucy that he could turn to Max with a grin. "You know I'm kidding."

Sebastian visibly vibrated with anger.

And Max spoke up as soon as the other man shut his arrogant mouth. "Actually, she's with me," Max said, pulling Lucy off of her seat and into the protection of his body.

Lucy stiffened, obviously surprised, but she made no move to edge away from his embrace.

Anthony's smile dimmed as he took in Max's proprietary stance, and to Max's surprise, Anthony took a step back. "I hear you boys are having some permit issues, and it's holding up construction on your restaurant."

"You heard wrong," Sebastian said, lying. But Max was glad he wasn't giving anything away to the competition.

"We're doing just fine," Max added.

"How about you worry about your own job and restaurant," Sebastian said, no longer feigning friendliness. "And keep your nose out of mine."

Meanwhile, Lucy snuggled in closer, and Max was more than ready to get the hell out of there and go home to finish what he'd started.

Chapter Eight

*L*ucy finished up a busy day at work, marveling at how much her life had changed. Another four weeks had passed. She sat at a big desk in her own office with its own sitting area in Midtown Manhattan. She'd even begun to decorate it and make it feel like hers, adding her favorite O'Keefe paintings and bright splashes of color, both in the pillows on the black leather sofa and chairs and the Orrefors vase and silk flowers in the center of the table. If a client came in, they would definitely sense her style.

As for Max and Sebastian, construction at the restaurant was well under way, and she had a small roster of her own clients at the firm already. She fit in well with the architects and designers there, met them for drinks, and worked on joint presentations as if she'd been there for years instead of only two months.

Her life in New York was busy. It was full and fun. Everything she hadn't had in LA, including and especially family. On Sunday, they were due to head over to Amanda and Decklan's apartment, and Lucy was excited. Although she'd seen Gabe, Isabelle, and Noah, Decklan and Amanda had been pretty much secluded since the wedding. Amanda claimed to have a stomach virus that just wouldn't go away. Lucy had a hunch it was more than that, and she was waiting for them to break the happy news. She just wished she was happier herself.

Oh, she was thrilled that her brothers were expanding their families. There was just that little voice inside her, the one she lived with, that told her nothing good lasted forever. That voice hadn't been around when her parents were alive. When Lucy was younger, she'd been much more easygoing and carefree. Nothing had bothered her, and why should it have? She'd been fortunate enough to have parents who loved her and brothers who looked out for her, and they didn't want for anything. But Lucy had taken everything for granted, including and most especially life itself.

Then, in an instant, her sense of safety and security were gone. Her parents, a memory. Her brothers had done their best to cushion the blow, but they couldn't minimize the loss of their parents or replace them, no matter how hard they'd tried or how much they loved her. Ever since, she'd anticipated bad news and loss, living life on the edge instead of fully immersing herself and being involved. This time back in New York was the closest she'd come to normal.

And she didn't trust it. She was waiting for the other proverbial shoe to drop. Yet every move she'd made in the last month had brought her closer to Max, bound them even more emotionally. He seemed to understand her. And maybe he did, considering he'd lost his wife the same way.

If she wanted to get inside his head too, all she had to do was ask him to explain. But that would bring them even closer, bind them more emotionally.

How much closer could you get? a little voice in her head mocked. She was already in so deep with the man. Yet she couldn't bring herself to change a thing. Not when they had a built-in expiration date anyway. When Savage in SoHo opened, Lucy and Max were over.

Max sat in the family room of Decklan and Amanda's one-bedroom apartment that Decklan had rented before he'd met his wife. Lucy had decorated for her brother and Amanda, choosing light, soothing colors that suited Amanda's personality. The room was small for a family gathering, but it was their home, and they were obviously happy.

They'd already been there for a while, sharing jokes, watching football, and enjoying a lazy, relaxing day with friends and family. Now the men sat in front of the television, football played on the large screen, and Gabe was talking. But Max's attention was more on the women in the kitchen . . . his woman in particular.

Lucy had seemed distracted all weekend, since she'd come home from work on Friday. She'd said she had a headache, and they'd stayed in, ordered food, and watched a movie on TV. Her mood had lasted all weekend despite the fact that she said her headache was better.

"Max, buddy, how's it going? I see you're making progress with my sister. You moved in almost immediately after my wedding," Decklan said, his gaze steady on Max.

"Really? I thought you wanted us together," Max said, not understanding Decklan at all. "Didn't we talk about this on the phone two months ago?" Because of course the minute Max had moved in with Lucy, Decklan had called, playing big brother.

Decklan groaned. "Sorry, man. Amanda hasn't been feeling well, and I'm on edge."

Max leaned forward, worried. "Is she okay?"

"Yeah." Decklan shook his head and laughed. "She's great, actually. Look, I'm all for you and my sister being a couple, but if she gets hurt, I might have to kill you. Then I'd be out a best friend." His tone was mild; the deadly warning look in his eyes was not.

Max grabbed the back of his neck and massaged the stiff muscles there. "If you have to worry about anyone getting hurt, it's me," he said, revealing more about his fears than he'd meant to.

"Is Lucy giving you a hard time?" Gabe asked, joining them, a glass of scotch in his hand.

Fuck. Max didn't need an in-depth probing into his emotions with the Dare brothers.

"Your sister is giving herself a harder time than anyone else is giving her. But I've got it under control." Or he was trying to control her feelings, and it wasn't working, Max thought, frustrated because this weekend he felt like he'd taken steps backward, not forward.

"It's time!" Amanda said, leading the women into the family room.

Isabelle walked over to Gabe and wrapped her arms around him, joining him on the sofa. Amanda did the same to Decklan. Lucy pulled up a chair from the dining room and sat by herself, proving his earlier point.

Max's gut was right. She was backing off. He gave her space for now, sensing she needed it. He'd crowd her later and try to figure out what was going on inside her head.

"So we have news," Amanda said, her tone rising with excitement.

"As if we haven't figured it out," Isabelle said under her breath, but her eyes twinkled with the same delight as Amanda's.

Lucy chuckled, telling Max that she, also, knew what was going on. But Max was clueless.

"I'm pregnant!" Amanda said, taking Max by surprise.

Apparently women's intuition had outsmarted him on this one, Max thought wryly. He watched Lucy as everyone congratulated the couple. Without a doubt, conflicting emotions crossed her face. Yes, she was happy about her brother and Amanda's pregnancy, but obviously she'd known the announcement was coming . . . and maybe that's what had her upset.

"There's more news," Decklan said, drawing Max's attention. "We're moving," he said, once everyone had retaken their seats. "Can't raise a family in this small place." He sounded every bit like a proud father to be, and Max was happy for his friend.

"Want to know the best part?" Amanda asked, practically glowing. "We bought a house near Gabe and Isabelle!" she said with a squeal of excitement.

"Playdates! Lunches!" Isabelle said, and the two women were off and running, discussing all the things they could do together once they lived close by.

The husbands watched, amused, but Max's attention was on Lucy . . . as she appeared to shrink back and into herself.

Time to get her out of here, Max thought. She couldn't live in her head anymore, and it was time for them to have a long, emotional talk. Unfortunately they couldn't leave now, not without being rude. But after dinner and before dessert, Max suggested they head home. Lucy immediately stood up to kiss her family good-bye, relief in her blue eyes.

He drove them back into the city, leaving the serious talk for once they were home.

Max parked in the garage beneath her building, but instead of heading upstairs to the apartment, he led her out of the garage and outside. She decided not to ask questions and see what he had in mind.

Her hand in his, they walked toward Central Park. The late-October weather had begun turning cold, and he pulled her close. Conflicting emotions churned inside her after Decklan and Amanda's announcements. She appreciated Max's strength and heat and curled into him as they walked.

He stopped at an empty bench, and they settled in, the slats beneath her thighs as cold as she felt inside.

"What are we doing here?" she asked.

"I wanted to go somewhere quiet."

Lucy bit down on her lower lip and met his obviously concerned gaze. He'd shaved early this morning, but he already had a shadow on his handsome face.

"Umm, why? Is something wrong?"

He grasped her hand, and her stomach flipped with nerves. "Because I noticed that lately something's bothering you . . . and when we were at your brother's, I realized what was going on."

"Oh? And what's that?" She straightened her shoulders, always wary and a little angry when he got into her head and read her mind.

"I'm doing this all wrong." He let out a groan. "Look, I shouldn't have to guess at what you're thinking or feeling. I'd rather you tell me what's going on," he said, frustration etched in his face. "Dammit, open up for once. Share your feelings with someone you know is going to understand."

"Fine. I knew Amanda was pregnant and they'd be telling us about it soon. And I'm happy for them. I am. But it's hard to watch them move on with their lives without me, okay?" Tears sprung to her eyes at the admission.

The truth hurt and made her feel guilty because she shouldn't be resentful of her brothers' happiness. She loved them and wanted them to be happy.

She blew out a shuddering breath, and Max waited patiently, his hand wrapped solidly around hers.

She swallowed past the lump in her throat and tried to explain. "It was easier for me to be alone and keep an emotional distance from the people I love when I was in California. It's harder being right here."

He wrapped a hand around hers. "Why do you feel like you have to keep that distance?" he asked, pushing for more answers.

She was past the point of holding back. "So I can't be hurt when they go away. Or don't have time for me anymore . . ."

"Or die," he finished for her in a soft voice.

"Or die." Her voice caught on that dreaded, hateful word.

He squeezed her hand tighter. "I think it's time I explain why I think I understand you so well."

She shivered, and it wasn't from the cool night air. He was about to bare his soul, and that scared her. She'd end up feeling more for him than she already did, if such a thing were possible. And if he delved into the similarities in their pasts, he would tell her how much he'd loved his wife and how losing her had destroyed him.

Hearing that would bring her back to her younger self. That girl had been filled with love and adoration, and she would have done anything to have Max in her life. But he'd married someone else, ripping her hopes and dreams out from under her. And that second loss had taught her to build her walls and keep them high, to keep everyone, even the people she loved, at a distance. She'd moved clear across the country to avoid his wedding, because losing him to another woman had felt like another death to her.

She didn't need to relive those feelings now.

Better to assure him she already understood. "I don't need you to explain. I know you lost your wife, Max. I'm sure you loved her very much, and that's kept you from having any long-term relationships since. And you figure that you understand the emotional barriers I use to keep people out. How's that for summing up why you think you can get into my head so easily?"

She folded her arms across her chest and deliberately slid farther away on the park bench, pain ripping through her at having to discuss all these things.

He shook his head and laughed, the sound wry and cynical. "You're not even close, princess."

That surprised her, and she couldn't stop herself from wanting to know more. "Tell me then."

He leaned one arm on the wooden slats behind him, staring at her with an expression she'd never seen before. Beneath the strong man she saw every day was one who'd also been hurt deeply.

"You know my parents took in foster kids, right?"

"I remember. We went to school together. But they didn't hang out with the neighborhood kids, so I never got to know them at all." She hadn't expected him to go back so far into his past, and she was immediately drawn in.

His jaw clenched tightly, the subject obviously not an easy one for him. "They were a rotating bunch. My mother would bend over backward trying to show them the love and affection they'd never had, but very few of them knew how to accept it. But my mom kept trying with them. Just not with me."

He paused, the silence heavy and weighted.

Her heart hurt at the revelation. He'd always been her brother's best friend, the guy who was always around. She'd never realized there was anything going on at home or wrong with his relationship with his mother. But she was younger then and wrapped up in her own feelings for the boy next door.

He drew a deep breath and went on. "The thing is, it wasn't always like that. Before we moved next door to you, we were a close family, just the three of us. Dad owned a restaurant near the small apartment we lived in, and it took both of my parents to keep it running. I used to work there after school, busing dishes and helping the chef in the kitchen when he'd let me."

Lucy smiled, wishing she could have seen a young Max learning the business and cooking.

"Dad was a good chef, and eventually someone approached him to partner and remodel. To make a long story short, the business took off, and we moved up in the world. Next door to you." He smiled at that, but his expression quickly soured.

"What happened?" she asked, leaning closer, wanting to know more.

"My mother had put her career in social work on hold to help in my father's restaurant, and as soon as he succeeded, she jumped back into her passion. She decided I'd already had all I needed in the way of emotional support, and the others needed her more."

His pain was palpable, that of a young boy stripped of everything he'd ever known for a reason that was cold and made no sense to a child. Hell, it made no sense to Lucy now, and she was an adult.

"And your dad?" she asked. Because he kept referring to his mother's shortcomings as a parent.

"My father was too wrapped up in the success of his business to notice or care what was going on at home." Max shrugged, as if that fact were unimportant, but Lucy knew he felt much more deeply than he let on.

She ought to know. She was an expert at covering up her feelings. "They were both wrong. You deserved so much more from them." Parents who loved and continued to love, to show their emotions and their feelings for their only child.

"I used to think it would have been better if I'd never known what it was like to be a real family. Then I wouldn't have felt the loss. Because once we moved next to you and everything changed, I felt like I'd had the foundations of my life ripped out from under me."

"Like a death," Lucy murmured, understanding immediately. He'd gone from two parents who doted on him and adored him to none.

"Exactly," he said, his voice gruff and filled with pain.

His big body shuddered, and she couldn't help but wrap her arms around him and give him the warmth and understanding he desperately needed, that he always shared with her. Because at this moment, he wasn't Max Savage, the strong man who tried to conquer her demons—he was the little boy who'd lost his parents.

"I never knew," she said, resting her head against his shoulder. She'd never realized how much they really did have in common. "But now I get why you can read me so well. Because we both suffered loss."

"I'm not sure you really do understand, because there's more." He straightened his shoulders, shrugging off the sadness of his childhood.

Suddenly Max Savage, dominant male, was back, with a determined gleam in his golden eyes and pride in his posture. He was the man who decided what he wanted and went after it, no holds barred.

Lucy shivered. "What do you mean?" she asked, suddenly wary because this Max had an agenda. And she was on it.

"I mean, I haven't tied everything together for you, but I will." He shifted toward her. "Yes, we both suffered loss. And you know how you keep the people you love at a distance? How you protect yourself by not letting yourself get too close, feel too much?" he asked, every word aimed at piercing that very armor she used to keep herself safe, because he knew her secrets.

"Yes?" she asked, unable to hide the tension shooting through her.

"Well, I learned that same lesson, and I learned it from my parents."

Lucy stared into his sexy gaze, lost and confused. He hadn't kept anyone at arm's length. In fact, he'd brought someone very, very close. "But you fell in love . . . and got married."

"No . . . and yes." He set his jaw, pausing in thought before continuing. "I think I need to backtrack in order to explain more about us."

"Us?"

He nodded. "At first you were just Decklan's pain-in-the-ass little sister."

Her lips curved in a smile at that description because she had been exactly that. She'd followed the boys around, wanting to be included, annoying them any way she could, usually just by her mere presence.

"Then, after your parents died, you were a sad, lost girl I wanted to look after and protect. But once you graduated from college and came home, I saw a different Lucy. You were a curvy, gorgeous woman."

"You noticed?" His compliment spread through her, warming her heart.

He nodded. "Oh, I noticed. And we spent a lot of time together then, and God, I wanted you." His body visibly shook at the memory, his eyes boring into hers, begging her to believe.

"You wanted me back then?" Lucy blinked in utter and complete shock. "I felt the same way," she whispered, the words falling unbidden from her lips. "But you never said a word. Never showed a sign!" She wanted to cry in frustration, knowing how different her life might have been if she'd been aware.

He reached out and stroked her cheek, his touch so welcome and sweet.

"You were too young then. You had your whole life ahead of you, and your brothers would have strung me up alive if I'd made a move at that point."

He spoke the truth. Still, her lips parted, ready to yell at him for giving in to what her brothers wanted instead of coming to her and offering them a chance.

He stopped her with his hand over her mouth, which he quickly dropped. "Don't say it. Because Decklan and Gabe weren't the only reason I kept my distance."

She shook her head, at a loss. "What other reason could there have been?"

Max groaned, aware that Lucy wouldn't be happy with the explanation. Still, it was time he laid it all out for her.

"I wanted you, Lucy. But I couldn't let myself have you." He pulled back and studied her wide-eyed, confused look. Yeah, this wouldn't go over well, but it was time they both faced the truth.

"Explain that."

"Look inside yourself, and you'll understand," he said, not meaning to be cryptic, merely honest.

She blew out a long breath and closed her eyes, her dark lashes sweeping down over her face, as she sat in silent, deep thought.

Finally she met his gaze. "You already told me you'd built your walls high, like me. Because of your parents."

"Yes." He nodded, keeping a close watch on her expressions as things were revealed.

He wanted to be able to catch every nuance and answer every question. He needed her to see that although she was afraid and resistant now, there was hope she could get past her fears.

"But . . . you married Cindy, so I'm not sure how high those walls could have been," she said, tipping her head to the side in confusion, even as her voice betrayed her hurt at the fact that he'd chosen someone else.

Her pained expression devastated him. It was only now, years later, with the wisdom of his own experience, that he realized how badly his choices had hurt her too.

He clenched his jaw and sought the easiest way to explain his actions. He finally settled on using her life as an example.

"Why were you with Lucas?" he asked, figuring that letting her draw the parallels would make this simpler.

She gnawed on her lower lip, a little quirk of hers he'd grown to recognize and enjoy.

"He was the safe choice," she whispered.

"Because?"

"I thought this was about your past, not mine." She narrowed her gaze, clearly not happy with what must have felt like an interrogation.

He smiled, hoping to reassure her. "They're tied together, princess. At least our reasons for doing things are. So bear with me, and I'll walk you through this."

She nodded jerkily. She obviously wasn't comfortable with this conversation, but she was letting him lead it, and he appreciated the trust it took for her to do so.

"Why was Lucas safe for you?" he asked again.

She glanced down, her gaze steady on her thighs.

Oh, he had no doubt she knew the answer. She just didn't want to admit it.

"Because there was no chance of me falling in love with him," she finally said, her voice even softer than before.

"Bingo." He reached out and tipped her chin up until she had no choice but to face him and the depth of emotion that had to be etched all over his face. He waited as she processed his words. He was with Lucy now. He had all the time in the world.

Lucy let out a shuddering breath, forcing her mind to focus, to draw all the right conclusions. And now that Max had, as he'd promised, tied things together, she caught up quickly.

"You didn't . . ." *love Cindy.* She cut herself off before she could finish the thought and decided not to put words in his mouth. "I mean . . . did you love Cindy?"

"Not enough." Max studied her with sad, guilt-ridden eyes. "And not the way I should have." He grasped her hands, his sudden hold on her too tight. "And certainly not the way I love you . . . and always have."

The words hit Lucy square in the gut . . . and in the heart. So many varied emotions tumbled around inside her that it was a wonder she could process them all. But somehow, she managed.

First came an overwhelming sense of relief—for the starry-eyed girl who'd loved Max Savage and believed he'd chosen someone he loved deeply and who wasn't her. Then anger because he'd deprived them of years of happiness, but how could she sustain anger when she, too, lived with the fear of loving so much and losing even more? And by now she realized she'd had years to perfect and hone the skill of keeping people she loved at a distance. It worked for her, preventing her from ever experiencing that aching sadness and grief again.

"Lucy, say something."

She couldn't. Because hot on the heels of those other emotions came fear and panic. "You . . . you love me?" She asked, horrified when every cell and molecule in her body knew she ought to be ecstatic and throwing herself into his arms.

"Always have, princess. It just took me years to get past the guilt and self-loathing I felt after Cindy died. I spent a lot of time losing myself in BDSM. And through the club, I met Dr. Daniel Carver. The guy considers himself the resident shrink there. If he likes you, he's going to make damn sure you don't hate yourself." He shrugged. "Guess I got lucky. The guy became a friend." His lips quirked upward, and his cheeks flushed with embarrassment at the admission.

She managed a smile, happy that Max had found peace after all these years. Too bad she couldn't say the same for herself.

But he'd ripped himself open for her, and she cherished the knowledge that he trusted her so intimately. She knew it couldn't have been easy for him to admit his weaknesses.

She ran her finger down his cheek, soaking in the feel of his scruff, the warmth of his skin beneath the outer cold. He was such a good man. And she was such a freaking mess.

"Do you understand the point behind this whole long-winded story?" he asked.

"Well, now I understand how and why you seem to understand me so well."

He smiled at that, his grin sexy to her, even if they were involved in a deep and serious conversation.

"That's only part of what I wanted you to take from it." He grasped her wrist in his hand, lowering it to his lap and holding on. "I also wanted you to understand that you don't have to be alone. You can let me in because I've been where you are." He brushed a strand of hair from her cheek with his free hand. "I won't let you get hurt."

She shivered, suddenly cold inside and out, and he immediately shrugged out of his jacket, wrapping it around her shoulders.

She pulled the sides closer, inhaling the masculine scent that made her feel deceptively safe. "That's just it, Max. You can't protect me from life."

"I can damn well try." And if all he needed was determination, she knew he'd accomplish his goal.

"If you'd come to me when I was younger and told me your feelings, I would have done anything to be with you." She sniffed, her nose stuffy, her eyes filling with tears. "But once you got engaged, it was like another death to me. I'd clung to this dream that you and I could be together, but you didn't want me—you wanted someone else. And I fled to California to get away from the pain . . . and from you."

She glanced at him through damp eyes to find his face stricken with both shock and pain.

"I didn't know."

She nodded. "How could you? We were two people who had deep feelings without acknowledging them. The timing was always wrong. Back then for you, and now for me. Just because you're ready doesn't mean I am."

He pulled her tight against him, and she cuddled into his warmth.

"I'm not giving up on you," he said gruffly.

"It's not fair to keep you going like this when I'm not sure I can give you what you need," she whispered.

He stroked her hair, long, soothing passes of comfort. "You will. I have enough faith for both of us."

Chapter Nine

*I*n the weeks that followed, Lucy put her all into trying to enjoy her life with Max and not live in fear. He'd opened his heart to her, and everything in her wanted to do the same. His life hadn't been as easy as she'd assumed, and she hurt for the little boy who'd latched on to *her* family because his own had been lacking.

Knowing he understood loss like she did and built protective defenses similar to hers allowed her to relate to him on a different level than she had before. But most of all, realizing how invested he always had been, her heart was lighter. For now it was the best she could do. That and be open to believing in the future, and over the last six weeks, she'd done just that.

Tonight she planned to surprise him by showing up at the restaurant and taking him out for dinner to celebrate the opening, which was planned for next week. She arrived at Savage in SoHo, where she felt like she'd lived while the furnishings had been delivered and installed.

Using her key, she walked through the front doors, struck, as always, by the changes from the dimly lit, gutted place she'd seen the first time. The dining area seated one hundred and twenty people in a bright room conveying the ambience of Barcelona. With wooden floors and expansive windows, ivy spread through a trellis on the walls, and suspended lighting from the ceiling, the inside evoked the feeling of the outdoors. Diners had their choice of pub-type or dining-height tables and chairs. Lucy was both proud and excited for the opening and potential success of the restaurant Max had created.

And though Sebastian was still having problems with his ex, he'd buckled down and worked on the menu, treating Max and Lucy to a sampling one night, and Lucy had left feeling certain they had a winner on their hands.

It looked like workers had left for the day and nobody was around.

"Max?" she called.

"Back here," he said, stepping out from the double kitchen doors. He wore a pair of jeans and a gray Henley, looking tired and yet utterly delectable at the same time.

She strode right up to him, rose onto her toes, and placed a kiss on his lips.

"What's that for?" he asked, his eyes twinkling with delight.

She was happy she could put that look there. "I thought I'd steal you away and take you for dinner. Looks like it's quiet anyway."

He nodded. "We finished up the hiring interviews, and Sebastian and I were going through the final choices. He got called away, so I was just wrapping up here."

"Great! Then my timing is perfect. Are you hungry?"

"I'm always hungry for you," he said, sliding a hand around her waist and pulling her close.

She cursed the need for a jacket, because she couldn't feel his hard body against hers. "Max, I was talking about food."

He grinned, and at that moment, his stomach grumbled loudly.

"That answers my question. I'm going to feed my man." Before she could walk off and lead him outside, he dipped his head, and his lips settled hard and firm on hers.

She loved his kisses. He always made her feel like there was nothing else in the world he'd rather be doing than kissing her, and she felt the same way. He delved deep, his tongue swirling around her mouth, thrusting in and out in a mimic of making love.

She moaned and threaded her hands in his hair while losing herself in the luxurious slide of his tongue and occasional nips on her lips. Because when it came to sex, Max was all about changing it up, surprising her, and most of all, making her feel good.

Suddenly the distinctive tone of his cell interrupted them, and Max broke the kiss, leaning his forehead against hers. "Shit."

She managed a laugh. "It's not like we could do anything more right now anyway." Even if her body was pulsing in all the right places, her sex softening, moisture dampening her panties. "Why don't you get it?"

He pulled the phone from his back pocket, frowned, and hit *end call*. His expression turned dark, and he shoved the phone back where it'd started. "Let's go," he muttered, his good mood clearly broken.

"Wait." She touched his arm. "Who was it?"

He met her gaze, the reluctance to answer obvious in his somber expression.

"Max?"

"My mother," he said and started for the front of the restaurant.

She blinked in shock. "Hey!"

He turned to face her.

"I didn't know you spoke to them." Other than that serious conversation between them, he'd never, not in all the time they'd been together, mentioned his parents.

"I don't." He raked a hand through his hair, tension vibrating from him in waves. "But they call. Sometimes."

"And do you always ignore them?" she asked, treading carefully over this sensitive subject.

He shrugged. "Why not? It's not like I have anything to say to them."

"But maybe they have something to say to you."

She, of all people, knew about things left unsaid. She hadn't had an argument with her parents before they'd died, but she'd been impatient to get back home from Gabe's graduation. She didn't remember telling them she loved them, something she regretted to this day. She didn't want Max to have similar regrets. Not when his parents were still alive and he could change their estrangement.

"They don't have anything to say that I want to hear," he muttered.

"I'm not sure that's true." Lucy pursed her lips and tried to come up with a way to help him deal with this past pain. "When was the last time you spoke to them?"

"When my father sold me his restaurant so they could retire. His partner had already passed away, and it was his to do with as he pleased. He needed the retirement money, and I'd already been in the business awhile, so I took out a loan and bought the place. We shook hands at the lawyer's office." A muscle jumped in his jaw, telling her how hard he must be clenching his teeth.

She reached out and smoothed her hand along his stubbled jaw. "Then don't you think a conversation between you all is long overdue?" she asked gently. "Obviously they've been reaching out, so they have something to say."

"I doubt it. And I can't imagine why they'd call. Guilt isn't something my parents feel, you know?"

Lucy wasn't convinced. "People change. Time passes, and they have a chance to rethink their actions. Aren't you a little curious?" she asked, not giving up.

"No."

"I don't believe you." She folded her arms across her chest and glared at him. "Aren't you the same man who told me you worked through your issues? So why wouldn't you want to do the same with your family? I'm not saying you have to forgive them. But you could at least hear what they want. Maybe you'll get some closure."

Lucy didn't know if closure was enough. She'd never know if she'd feel any differently about losing her parents if she'd had advance warning, or if she'd at least been able to say what was always in her heart. But she was pushing hard to make sure Max had that opportunity now.

He pinched the bridge of his nose and groaned. "I'll think about it."

"I'll go with you," she offered. If he could find . . . if not a relationship, then some measure of peace, he deserved at least that.

He held on to her gaze and finally nodded. "Okay then."

She smiled. "Okay." He grasped her hand and led her outside, locking up behind them.

They went to dinner at their favorite Mexican restaurant near the apartment and relaxed over fajitas and tequila for him, a frozen margarita for her. No touchy subjects came up, and they just enjoyed.

A little while later, they returned home. Lucy headed for the master bathroom. She washed up and slipped on her favorite negligee, a red chemise with black lace and a bow where the cleavage dipped low, before joining Max.

He sat in bed, back propped against the pillows. A sheet covered his tented erection, and his bare chest beckoned to her from across the room.

"C'mere, princess," he said in a gruff voice she had no problem obeying.

She stepped across the hardwood floor and onto the area rug surrounding the bed before sliding onto the mattress and into his arms.

He pulled her on top of him, and she sat up, straddling his hips. "Hey," she said, looking into his eyes.

"Hey yourself." She wriggled her lower body until his cock settled against the aching space between her thighs.

He wrapped a hand around her and cupped her ass cheek in one hand. "No underwear."

"Nope."

"Trying to tell me you're in the mood?" Max asked her.

She treated him to what she hoped was a sinful smile. "I'm always in the mood for you," she said in a version of his earlier comment to her.

She eased herself off him and settled on one side, then slowly slid the covers down and off his straining erection.

"Lucy," he said, a distinct warning in his voice.

"Oh, are you against a blow job?" she asked.

He let out a low growl. "You're going to pay for being impertinent."

She laughed, her sex already tingling. "I hope so," she said, as she gripped his cock and licked her tongue over the head in a teasing gesture.

He slid his hand across her back and up to her neck, gripping her tightly. She moaned and closed her mouth around his shaft, pulling him in deep.

"Oh, fuck," he muttered, his hips jerking upward, forcing his cock to the back of her throat.

She managed to swallow around him and continue. She held on to his hard length and worked her mouth up and down, lubricating him and pumping her hand as she worked to arouse him further and take him to the brink.

His grip on her neck never eased, and the low groans coming from his throat served to heighten both her sense of power and her own excitement and need. But she was wholly focused on him and determined to make him lose his mind. She slid her mouth up and down, alternating using her tongue, tasting his salty essence, and teasing him with light grazing of her teeth.

He suddenly tugged on her hair. "I'm gonna come, Lucy." His voice sounded gruff and harsh.

She appreciated the warning, but she wasn't about to stop now. She tightened her grip and renewed her determination, sliding her tongue beneath the sensitive head until he bucked his hips and his come exploded in her mouth.

She swallowed what she could, knowing some dripped down her face. When he collapsed, muscles releasing their tension, she lifted her gaze and rubbed the remaining wetness on his thigh. He could just clean it off in the shower, she thought, highly pleased with herself.

"Get over here," he said gruffly.

She eased herself up and over his body, her own still tingling with need. He gripped her hips and pulled her up until she straddled his face, her pussy hovering above his mouth.

"Max," she murmured, a mixture of embarrassed and uncomfortable. Sex with Lucas—heck, sex with the men in her past—had been quick and missionary. Everything with Max had been exciting and new. But this . . . she was so open to him.

"Relax, princess. Now ease yourself down."

When she didn't respond immediately, he gripped her hips harder. She moaned and did as he asked. Next thing she knew, she was lost in sensation, his mouth on her sex.

She grabbed on to the headboard, unable not to rock her hips back and forth as he licked and sucked her into oblivion. His talented tongue lapped at her lips, up one side and down the other, before darting inside her. She moaned and pushed against him, barely aware when she took one hand and rubbed it over her sensitive clit. Pleasure mounted quickly, faster than ever before.

Between the friction of his mouth and the pressure of her finger, she detonated quickly, her entire body shaking and succumbing to pleasure and stars exploding behind her eyes as she rode out wave after wave of the most intense climax. She collapsed beside him, barely aware when he pulled her into his arms and into the protective curve of his body.

A little while later, they showered, taking the time for a luxurious round of making love under the hot, steamy water. And she couldn't call it anything less than that. Nothing she did with Max fell under one category only. He wasn't just her lover. He wasn't just her best friend. He wasn't just anything.

He was everything.

She loved him despite having done everything in her power to avoid feeling this way. And now? She'd have to deal with the fallout.

Max hadn't thought he'd visit the house of his adolescence ever again. Yet somehow, because Lucy had convinced him, he was here to talk to his parents. He'd known today would be tough for him. But Lucy was right about regrets, and he didn't want to be coming back here with things he should have done haunting him. As they approached the old neighborhood where she'd grown up with her parents, her silence told him that he wasn't the only one facing the past today.

Gabe had sold the house next door to his after Lucy graduated from college, and as far as he knew, she hadn't returned since. As he parked out front, he glanced to the side, noting her complexion had turned pale. Apparently she wasn't any more ready to face the past than he was.

He turned off the engine, and she hurried out of the car, rushing over to grab his hand, taking over . . . taking care of him. If it meant she was putting her own painful thoughts out of her mind, he'd let her take the lead.

Max rang the doorbell and met Lucy's gaze for a brief second before the door opened and his mother stood before him. She'd aged. There were fine lines in her face that hadn't existed the last time he'd seen her, and there was a light sprinkling of gray in her brown hair. His mother had never been one to overly worry about personal appearance, and that hadn't changed. No hair dye or heavy makeup for her.

"Max," she whispered, almost as if she couldn't believe he was standing there.

"Mom."

She blinked back tears, and he didn't know what to make of the change. In this older woman, he saw signs of the mom he'd grown up with in that small apartment, before she'd let her job overtake her family.

"You remember Lucy," he said, his hand on the small of her back.

"Hi, Mrs. Savage."

"Loretta," she corrected her.

"Loretta. It's nice to see you again," Lucy said.

"Come in, come in. It's cold outside." She ushered them into the house, which was still decorated the same way Max remembered. Not overly ornate but too fancy for his taste—especially as a teenage boy prone to running, not walking—and for a houseful of foster kids.

A little while later, they sat with both of Max's parents on the porch they'd enclosed to create a sun-room. His father, Victor, looked pale, and though the room was heated, he had a blanket over his legs.

"Dad, are you okay?" Max asked him, realizing his father had aged as well. His complexion was sallow, his shoulders hunched, and he lacked the strong-as-a-bull appearance Max had always associated with his dad.

"Just some reaction to chemo."

Lucy sucked in a startled breath, and Max felt as if he'd been punched hard. He wanted to double over, but he remained upright. "What kind?"

"Lymphoma, but it's under control."

His father had always been a straight shooter, and Max believed him. Max nodded slowly. "That's good then."

Max felt sad for the years that had passed, worried about the man who'd raised him, and though there was some guilt for not returning their calls, a part of him was still that hurt boy they'd all but turned their backs on.

"Is that why you've been calling?" he asked, looking at his mother, who sat by Victor's side.

"No, actually we've been dealing with the cancer on and off for a while now," Loretta said. "It makes you look back on your life. Reflect."

Beside him on the sofa, Lucy slid a hand into his as he listened, stunned by the fact that there was more to this visit than letting him know his father was sick.

"Max, I loved being your mom."

"Could have fooled me," he said, the bitter words escaping before he could censor his reply.

His mother rose and walked over, then knelt down beside him, the pain in her eyes a tangible thing. "I hated working the restaurant. I never wanted you to know that. I never wanted your dad to know that. I wanted the career I went to school for, but I loved my family. I wanted the restaurant to succeed so your dad would be happy. So we'd have money so you'd have the things you needed and you wouldn't want for anything."

Max gripped his hands together in his lap, knowing Lucy was there, by his side. "We didn't need money, Mom. We needed each other," he said gruffly, uncomfortable because they'd never had these kinds of serious conversations. At least not back then, when it would have helped. When it would have mattered.

She dipped her head once, acknowledging his point before meeting his gaze. "You always were such a little adult, a self-sufficient child." She smiled, shaking her head. "I mean, at ten years old, you could cook better than I could."

He shook his head, unable not to laugh. "I inherited that talent from dad."

His father, who had been watching in silence, smiled at that comment. But Max had the distinct impression they'd already discussed how this talk would go, that his mother would lead. And given that she'd been the one to make the major changes in their family's past, maybe it was the right thing to do.

"When the restaurant took off and our lives changed, I grasped on to the opportunity to live my dream, to help kids in need."

"I never begrudged you that. Hell, I never begrudged them the chance to start over. I just didn't think I'd be the one left out in my own house. In my own family." Max was mortified to find his voice cracking on the piece of truth that always had the power to break his heart.

"I know. I handled things all wrong. I got all wrapped up in what they needed, in my do-good career I'd put on hold. I didn't even realize I messed up my family until the kids were gone, you were gone . . . and nobody came back anymore."

"Because you didn't create a family, Mom. You gave them a house, you gave them the things they needed. You told me I already had those things so I didn't need more. But I think you forgot the most important thing in the mix. Love."

"I know that now, and I'm sorry. When I thought I was going to lose your father, it was all I could do to put one foot in front of the other. Once I realized he was going to be okay and I really looked at my life . . . I wasn't proud of what I saw. I've missed you. So much."

He felt Lucy beside him, her strength giving him more, allowing him to deal with this piece of his past. He really had thought it was all behind him, but she was right. How did you ever leave your parents without closure? And now that he was here, seeing how his father was ill, his mother seemingly sorry, he had to ask himself . . . did he really want to go on without them in his life? Did he want to live with regrets?

"Can you forgive me?" his mother asked.

He rose to his feet, helping her do the same. "You're my mother. I'm not going to hold a grudge for the rest of my life." It wouldn't help him now. "I don't know what kind of relationship we'll have, but we can try."

She released the tears she'd been holding in and wrapped her arms around him tightly. "Thank you."

He patted her awkwardly on the back, knowing this was just a tiny step. There would be other awkward get-togethers in the future before the rift ever really mended.

She pulled away, and he walked over to his father, who had stood up to join them. "I wasn't much better, son. Not paying attention to what was going on at home, focusing on work to the exclusion of my family."

There wasn't much to say to that, so he merely hugged the older man, noticing how frail he felt to the touch. He was happy he'd made this trip, glad he'd listened to Lucy.

He turned to find her, to tell her, to thank her, but she'd disappeared.

Lucy slipped out of the room and left the house, making her way to the backyard next door, where she'd grown up. She sat in the ultramodern jungle gym the new owners must have erected, and swung back in a swing. A layer of sadness filtered over the pleasure she'd found in watching Max reach a tentative sense of peace with his parents, something she'd never had the chance to do. It made her miss her family even more.

When she'd offered to come here with Max, she hadn't given a thought to how she'd feel returning to the neighborhood. Now she knew. Her heart hurt.

She'd come to terms with losing her parents years ago, but being here reminded her of what she'd had and lost. Of what she could have with Max . . . and the fear of being destroyed should something go wrong.

"Excuse me . . ." A woman approached her, walking toward her warily. "Umm, can I help you?" She stopped a few feet away, obviously afraid Lucy was an unhinged female in her yard.

She rose to her feet. "I'm sorry. I'm Lucy Dare, and I'm visiting the Savage family next door."

"And you just thought you'd play in our backyard?" the blonde asked, confused.

"I used to live here," Lucy explained. "I grew up in your house. I'm sorry I scared you."

The woman's shoulders dropped in relief. "I'm Carrie Sanders. We bought this house two years ago."

"It's changed hands a few times then," Lucy mused.

Carrie nodded. "The last owners were in the financial sector. The husband was transferred to Hong Kong."

"Mom!" a little voice yelled from the house.

She shot Lucy a wry smile. "That's me. I've got to be going."

"Don't worry. I'll leave too. No worries about the strange lady in your backyard."

"Lucy!" Max called, the concern in his voice clear.

"And that's my cue anyway. Nice meeting you," Lucy said.

"Same." Carrie glanced at her, watching as she walked out of the yard, probably relieved.

Not that Lucy blamed her. She had a family in the house to protect.

Lucy rubbed her arms with her hands, feeling the chill in the air down to her bones. Or maybe it was the chill of memories. She wasn't sure.

She met up with Max on the driveway of his parents' house. "There you are! Jesus. You scared me, disappearing like that."

"Sorry," she murmured. "I didn't mean to worry you. I just took a walk next door."

He narrowed his gaze. "I would have gone with you if you'd asked."

She smiled but wasn't feeling any lightness at all. "I know. But you were busy with your parents, and I figured I'd get it over with, you know?"

He grasped her hands in his and held on with all his strength. "I do know. Which is why I wish you'd waited for me."

"Everything okay with your mom?" she asked, sticking to his life, not hers.

"We made a start, thanks to you. I never would have come here if you hadn't pushed."

"I really am glad, Max. Life is short. You don't know how much time you have left. Better to make peace with the past while you still can. And maybe have a future with them that's better. For all of you."

"Lucy, you know I'm here for you, right?"

"I know." And she did. She just couldn't *feel* anything since visiting her old house.

"No, princess. I'm *here*. No matter how tough things are, I'm not going anywhere, ever. Because I love you." His amber eyes met hers.

Everything she'd ever needed and wanted, she found in his handsome face, concerned expression, and honest, from-the-heart words. He'd told her he loved her before, when he'd explained his own life and bared his soul. He hadn't pushed for her to say the words back and hadn't repeated them again until now.

She loved him too. With every fiber of her being, and she sensed he knew it. But she couldn't bring herself to say so out loud. First, because she just couldn't find her emotions. They were locked inside her, frozen in ice, in the pain of loss and the fear of facing that emptiness again. And also because if she told him she loved him, she'd make it real. Put it out there in the universe and risk life laughing at her. At the futility of allowing herself to be happy, when it could all disappear again so easily.

"Max." She squeezed his hands tightly, the best she could do to express her feelings at the moment.

"I know, princess. You'll say it when you're ready."

Except she feared she never would be . . . and he'd get tired of waiting.

Chapter Ten

"So I have the walk-through with the inspector, a couple of meetings at the restaurant, and then I'll come by and steal you away from work," Max said, speaking to Lucy on his cell. "Sound good?"

"I'll do my best to get out early," she said, sounding distracted. He understood. They'd both been extremely busy lately, and this morning she'd had an early meeting at the office.

"Enjoy lunch with the girls. I'll call you later."

"Sounds good," she said, disconnecting the call.

Isabelle and Amanda were coming into the city to visit Lucy and take her to lunch, and as far as Max was concerned, it couldn't come soon enough. She needed to talk to someone about her feelings, and if it wasn't him, maybe one of her sisters-in-law could get through to her.

Max had a healthy ego, but even he was worried about how far into herself Lucy had withdrawn since the visit to their old neighborhood. She took self-protection to the extreme, and though he'd love to deal with it now, he didn't have time to focus on his personal life. Not with the opening night for Savage in SoHo creeping up in a few short days.

Despite the hassles with the permits and the usual bullshit with the contractors, in the end, Max was damned proud of the result. Hiring Lucy had been the key to pulling the ambience together, and he couldn't wait for the customers to visit and see for themselves. He'd even invited his parents to attend, snagging them a table despite already being booked solid for all seatings that evening.

Although it had only been a few days since his visit home, both his mother and father called each day, proving to Max that they were intent on mending the rift between them. How could he deny any of them the opportunity to have the family they used to have?

Knowing he had Lucy to thank only made him more determined to free her of her own ghosts, even if he had to introduce her to his old friend, Dr. Daniel Carver, at the BDSM club. He hadn't visited the place in ages, but he would if it meant getting Lucy's head where she needed it to be for a healthy, happy life. And he would, as soon as the restaurant was up and running.

Right now, though, he was due to meet an inspector from the health department for a final walk-through, and he'd been held up by a phone call about delivery issues from another location. Finally free, he grabbed his keys from the bowl on the counter in the apartment hallway and rushed out the door, opting for a cab as the quickest way of getting downtown.

No sooner had he settled into the back seat and given the driver the address than his phone rang with a number he didn't recognize. "Hello?"

"Max? It's Sebastian."

"Hey, man. You on your way to meet the inspector? I need you to hold down the fort for a few minutes. I had a call that ran long, and I'm running late."

"Umm, no. You're my one phone call, so listen up. I've been arrested."

Max all but slapped his hand against his forehead. "What the fuck?"

"It's a misunderstanding, I swear. Gia's lost her mind, and she's accused me of assault. But I need you to call my lawyer and bail me out. I'm at the Fifth Precinct."

Max leaned against the plastic seat of the cab and groaned. Sometimes he regretted getting involved with the reality TV star who had more drama in his life than any normal person dealt with in a lifetime.

This was one of those moments. "And what am I supposed to do about the inspector?"

"He's a decent guy. Just call and reschedule."

"Reschedule?" Max yelled. "We're opening in three days!"

"Gotta go," Sebastian said. "I owe you one," he added before disconnecting the call.

Max redirected the cab driver to the precinct and called the inspector, leaving a suck-up apologetic message about having to reschedule. These guys could be difficult, and their time was tight. He'd have to tap-dance well to get the man back in before the opening, or it wouldn't happen.

Then Max looked up Sebastian's lawyer's phone number, which he had on his cell thanks to their legal work with the restaurant. The guy wasn't a criminal attorney, but he'd find Sebastian a good one. And though Max would prefer to go through with the inspection now, he knew he'd better make sure he had liquid funds with which to bail out his chef instead.

Because the restaurant's success hinged on Sebastian being sprung from jail and available to cook on opening night.

Exhausted after a long day of meetings, Lucy walked into her apartment and tossed her oversized workbag onto the couch, collapsing beside it in relief. She was supposed to have had lunch with her sisters-in-law, but Noah had a fever, causing Isabelle to cancel, and Amanda had begged off because she was nauseous. Again.

Lucy shivered, the very idea of pregnancy at this point a scary concept. *Thank you, Amanda*, she thought wryly, although she felt awful for her sister-in-law. Still, Lucy had to admit that the change of plans turned out to be a blessing in disguise, since she'd been handed two new unexpected clients. She'd eaten lunch in the office, barely taking a break all day. She'd still gotten out a little early and texted Max, letting him know she'd be home when he finished up at the restaurant instead of at work.

All she wanted to do was chill out for a while and relax, already thinking about ordering in dinner instead of going out. She lifted her feet onto the table and grabbed the remote, turning on the big-screen television. The familiar anchors on her favorite channel were discussing the weather, which had undergone a sudden chill.

She closed her eyes and sighed, her thoughts immediately traveling to Max. And their lives together. And Lucy's sucky attitude ever since visiting home. Before then, she'd been . . . on the road to happy. She'd let old memories derail what they'd found. It was so easy for her to fall into those old habits and fears. *Too easy*, she thought. Max was the best thing that had ever happened to her, and he deserved to know it.

He was opening a restaurant this week. The least she could do was support him through it, be as excited and proud as he was, and be a true partner. Like her mother had been to her father, she realized, her eyes snapping open at the thought. Ever since they'd died so unexpectedly, when Lucy thought of her parents, she thought of loss.

It had been a long time, if ever, since she'd thought of the marriage and love they'd shared, the partnership they'd forged as a couple, and the family they'd successfully raised. How else could Gabe have stepped in and made sure she graduated high school and then college, being the parent she needed? How had both her siblings managed to overcome their hurt and fears to marry women they loved and start families? And if they were strong enough to do it, why wasn't she?

She rubbed her hands over her eyes, trying to pull all her thoughts together into something that made sense for her, for the future.

One thing she knew for sure: her brothers were going to make wonderful fathers. They'd proven their abilities with her. And as soon as she could, she intended to thank them for all they'd done for her to help her grow up healthy, whole . . . and loved. They needed to hear her tell them how happy she was that they'd found peace, contentment, and the type of family they'd had growing up. And she wanted to be a part of it, the fun-loving aunt who their kids looked forward to seeing. Not the eccentric one who hid away, afraid of her feelings. Who said she couldn't make progress? she thought wryly.

Her stomach chose that moment to rumble, and she frowned. "Where are you, Max?"

She picked up her phone to see if he'd replied. Still nothing, and she frowned. It wasn't like him not to keep in touch, especially if they had plans.

She called Sebastian, wondering if maybe he had information on the final inspection and Max's whereabouts, but his cell also went directly to voice mail. *Weird.*

Five more minutes, and she'd order up a pizza for delivery, she thought and settled in to watch TV while she waited.

The news switched to coverage on an explosion that had occurred. She frowned. Lately there had been more than a few explosions in the city—some gas related, some arson, while in others, the cause was still under investigation. But given the tenor of the news, she wasn't surprised.

She raised the volume on the television to find out where the explosion had occurred.

What appears to be a gas explosion reduced the building to rubble. The restaurant, Savage in SoHo, belonged to restaurateur Max Savage with head chef reality TV star Sebastian Del Toro.

Her heart began to race, and panic set in. Lucy frantically hit Max's name on her screen, but she couldn't get past the voice mail. Her phone rang, and her brother's name flashed.

"Gabe, help me. It's Max, I—"

"I know. And Decklan's already in the city, sweetheart," Gabe said in a strong voice, interrupting her hysteria. "Where are you?"

She pulled in long breaths. "My place. Our apartment, Max's and mine," she said, her voice rising.

"Okay, sit tight. I'm going to let him know where to come get you. Everything's going to be okay, Lucy. You hear me?" Gabe asked. Gabe, the one who'd been her voice of reason for as long as she could remember.

Tears were falling, and she couldn't breathe. All she could think of was Max. He'd had back-to-back meetings scheduled at the restaurant. The inspection. A few appointments. He'd been there all day. Which meant he'd been there when the explosion had happened.

Nausea threatened, and she jumped up from the couch. She couldn't just sit around and do nothing, waiting for her brother. She grabbed her bag and ran out of the apartment. She banged on the elevator button, impatient, frustrated, and so damned scared. By the time she made it to the street and scanned for a cab, it had started drizzling, and between the light rain and the hour of the day, taxis were scarce.

Uber. She flipped over her phone, her hands shaking as she tried to swipe and find the app, and her phone slipped and fell to the ground.

"Dammit!"

"Ms. Dare," the doorman said, joining her by the curb. He bent down and retrieved her cell, handing it to her. "Can I help you?"

"I need . . . I need . . ." She couldn't get the words out, and then she heard a familiar voice call her name.

"Lucy!"

She turned toward her brother's voice and ran for his police car, jerking the door open and stumbling into the front seat. "Decklan, do you know anything?" she asked.

He reached out and grabbed her hand. "I know that some-one was taken to the hospital, but I don't know who. And I don't know the extent of their injuries."

She swallowed hard. "Okay." Not being alone helped quell the panic.

"I have ears at the site," Decklan assured her. "So if Max shows up there or is found, I'll get a heads-up immediately. In the meantime, we can check out the hospital."

She thanked her lucky stars that her brother was a cop with access to the most up-to-date information. "Let's do that," she said, feeling better now that they had a plan. "Maybe Max is there, and he lost his phone. Then he wouldn't be able to call, right?"

"Right." Decklan spoke in a strong, certain tone, and Lucy took comfort from that.

If her brother wasn't jumping to the worst possible conclu-sion, then neither would she.

She twisted her fingers together in her lap as Decklan swung out into rush-hour traffic. Getting from the Upper East Side to downtown Manhattan in the rain was going to be a long trek, and she mentally prepared herself for the trip.

Unfortunately she couldn't stop her rampaging thoughts, and those weren't pleasant. She didn't want to think about Max being injured or . . . dead. But having been in this posi-tion before, rushing to a hospital, waiting on word, she knew the worst-case scenario was, in fact, possible. Would she be forced to relive her ultimate nightmare? Could God, fate, the universe be that cruel?

Why not, when she'd been *that* stupid?

Holding back when all he did was give, allowing her fears to control everything she did and said. Or . . . didn't say. Like *I love you.*

She ran a shaking hand through her hair.

"Hey, sis. Max is one tough son of a bitch. He's going to be okay. There's no way he wouldn't do everything he could to come back to you."

She swallowed hard. "I know. But why? I've given him so much less than what he's given me. I couldn't even say 'I love you' back. He deserves better."

"Lucy, you've been through a huge trauma at a critical age. Don't you think maybe you're being too hard on yourself?" her brother asked, eyes focused on the road as he wove in and out of traffic.

She shook her head. "No, I don't. Because I realize now, if Max is gone? I didn't save myself hurt and heartache! I cost myself more."

All those regrets she'd cautioned Max about having toward his family? She was sitting on a big whopping pile of those now, and she only had herself to blame.

"I love him, and he needs to know. He has to know." She swiped at the tears running down her cheeks.

Her brother merely squeezed her hand and continued his winding through the city streets, trying to get to the hospital as soon as possible. Meanwhile, Lucy prayed that one way or another, she'd find Max, and when she did, that he wasn't too badly hurt. No matter what, though, she wasn't leaving his side.

She refused to think of any other alternative.

Max's head pounded, his throat felt raw, and his body ached like he'd been thrown to the concrete. Because he had been. One minute he was walking into Savage in SoHo, and the next he'd been airborne. He didn't remember much afterward, but now he had oxygen in his nose, an IV in his arm, and pain radiating everywhere. He closed his eyes because it hurt to open them, and let everything drift away.

He wasn't sure how much time had passed when he heard a loud voice. A female voice and a familiar one at that. "If Max Savage is in that room, I want to see him!"

"I'm sorry, but you said yourself you aren't family."

"Well, I will be."

"Not good enough. He's—"

"It's good enough for me. And it'll be good enough for him if you'd just step aside—"

"Lucy?" Max ripped the oxygen from his nose, and, ignoring the throbbing in his head, he yelled again. "Lucy!"

"You see? He wants me."

Yes, Max thought, he damned well did.

The curtain parted, and Lucy stormed through, coming up to his bed and meeting his gaze. "Max. Thank God."

A nurse hurried in behind her, but Max waved her away. He didn't give a shit how much he hurt; his focus was on Lucy.

She wrapped her arms around his and laid her head on his chest. "I saw the news, and I thought . . . I mean, you were supposed to be inside the restaurant, and you weren't answering your phone. I thought . . ." She burst into tears, sobbing against him, her tears dampening his skin.

His arms were sore, but he laid one hand across her back, aware of her shaking shoulders.

"Apparently I'm hard to get rid of," he said wryly. But he knew how badly this experience must have screwed with her head, not to mention her emotions. He wondered how much work he had ahead of him to bring her back emotionally now.

"Don't joke." She sniffed and raised her head. Her eyes were red and puffy, her face splotchy, and yet she'd never looked more beautiful to him.

He was so damned lucky to be here with her now. And he had Sebastian to thank. If the man hadn't required bail money, Max would have been inside the restaurant instead of just arriving there when the explosion happened.

"Lucy—"

"Don't speak. Not a word. Just rest. I'll do all the talking."

Sounded good to him. Whatever she had to say, he wanted to hear. As long as it wasn't good-bye. Because if almost losing him had convinced her to give up on them . . .

"I love you," she said, the words sounding thought out and sure.

He blinked, stunned because he'd thought he'd never hear that phrase from her beautiful lips. Hell, he'd convinced himself he could live without hearing it, if it meant still having her in his life. He knew now, as she offered all of herself, that he'd been wrong. Having only part of her would never have been enough.

"I love you too, princess," he said, his voice gruff.

"I can't believe I thought keeping my emotions locked up would keep me from being hurt." She treated him to a smile, but clearly she was still beating herself up. "If I'd lost you, I'd regret all the things I never said, the love I never showed you. I've been selfish, and I'm so sorry." Her tears flowed freely once more.

"There's nothing to apologize for. You couldn't help your reaction to something so vital being taken away from you. Of all people, I understand." He drew a breath, doing his best not to cough, cause his head to pound harder, and send that nurse running back in here. "I hurt Cindy in an effort to protect myself. I'm sure as hell not going to judge you. But promise me one thing."

"What's that?"

"We put it all behind us and enjoy life from here on out."

"That I can do. Will you do something for me?" she asked on a shaky breath.

"Name it."

She lifted his hand, threading their fingers together. "Marry me. I don't want to waste any more time being afraid of what could be taken away from me. I want to know I'm celebrating the life I do have."

Max wondered if he'd lost his hearing in the blast. "Did you just say marry you?" he asked incredulously.

She nodded, eyes wide and uncertain.

"Yes."

Her lips lifted, her smile wide and real.

"But know you're going to pay for asking," he said in a stern voice, though inside he felt light and incredibly happy.

"What? Why?"

"Because I'm the one in control, remember?"

"In the bedroom, not out of it!" she sputtered.

He chuckled but ignored her proclamation, figuring she needed a reminder of all the things that worked well in their relationship. "Since you tried to take that control away from me, I'm going to make sure you feel the sting of my hand on your ass, princess."

Her mouth parted in a soft *oh*, and her eyes dilated as she thought through his statement . . . and realized she wanted him to take back those reins. "Fine," she said on a huff. "As long as you're mine, I don't mind letting you think you're in control."

He burst out laughing at that, which did cause his head to pound, and he groaned out loud.

"Max, lie still!" Lucy said, this time her tone brooking no argument.

Which was exactly what he appreciated about their relationship—the give and the take. "Whatever you say."

She pulled up a chair and leaned in close. "How bad is the restaurant?" she asked.

"It's gone."

She closed her eyes and sighed.

"Doesn't matter. Things can be replaced. It's people that matter."

"Amen. And whatever happens, I'll be there to help you rebuild."

He ran a tired hand over her long tresses. "I'm counting on it," he said on a yawn. "I'm counting on you." His heavy eyelids wanted to close, and he stopped fighting the exhaustion.

"You can count on me," he heard Lucy say. "Now and forever, Max."

He believed her.

Epilogue

One year later

New York Post
Page Six

Savage in SoHo, the newest tapas restaurant in lower Manhattan and brainchild of restaurateur Max Savage and acclaimed reality TV star chef Sebastian Del Toro opened to accolades and five-star ratings this past week. Celebrities abounded at the grand opening. The inside of the restaurant evoked the feeling of the streets of Barcelona, the designer, Lucy Savage, recreating the original interior that was destroyed last year in an act of arson, courtesy of a jealous competitor, Anthony Abbadon, who took outrageous reality TV too far. Abbadon pled guilty and is currently serving time.

Many speculated Savage would scrap the project, especially since his chef was dealing with criminal charges of assault and battery at the time. Instead, he stood by his longtime friend. Del Toro was eventually acquitted of all charges, and Savage continues his Midas touch. After the grand opening, Max Savage and his wife, Lucy, left on a delayed honeymoon in Bali, where they are expected to be in seclusion for two weeks. Enough time for babies? Only time will tell . . .

Want more Dare family stories?
Read the Dare to Love series!

Dare to Love Series

Book 1: *Dare to Love* (Ian & Riley)
Book 2: *Dare to Desire* (Alex & Madison)
Book 3: *Dare to Touch* (Olivia & Dylan)
Book 4: *Dare to Hold* (Scott & Meg)
Book 5: *Dare to Rock* (Avery & Grey)
Book 6: *Dare to Take* (Tyler & Ella)

NY Dares Series

Book 1: *Dare to Surrender* (Gabe & Isabelle)
Book 2: *Dare to Submit* (Decklan & Amanda)
Book 3: *Dare to Seduce* (Max & Lucy)

Turn the page to start reading the *Dare to Love* excerpt!

Excerpt from *Dare to Love* by Carly Phillips. All rights reserved.

Chapter One

Once a year, the Dare siblings gathered at the Club Meridian Ballroom in South Florida to celebrate the birthday of the father many of them despised. Ian Dare raised his glass filled with Glenlivet and took a sip, letting the slow burn of fine scotch work its way down his throat and into his system. He'd need another before he fully relaxed.

"Hi, big brother." His sister Olivia strode up to him and nudged him with her elbow.

"Watch the drink," he said, wrapping his free arm around her shoulders for an affectionate hug. "Hi, Olivia."

She returned the gesture with a quick kiss on his cheek. "It's nice of you to be here."

He shrugged. "I'm here for Avery and for you. Although why you two forgave him—"

"Uh-uh. Not here." She wagged a finger in front of his face. "If I have to put on a dress, we're going to act civilized."

Ian stepped back and took in his twenty-four-year-old sister for the first time. Wearing a gold gown, her dark hair up in a chic twist, it was hard to believe she was the same bane of his existence who'd chased after him and his friends until they relented and let her play ball with them.

"You look gorgeous," he said to her.

145

She grinned. "You have to say that."

"I don't. And I mean it. I'll have to beat men off with sticks when they see you." The thought darkened his mood.

"You do and I'll have your housekeeper short-sheet your bed! Again, there should be perks to getting dressed like this, and getting laid should be one of them."

"I'll pretend I didn't hear that," he muttered and took another sip of his drink.

"You not only promised to come tonight, you swore you'd behave."

Ian scowled. "Good behavior ought to be optional considering the way he flaunts his assets," he said with a nod toward where Robert Dare held court.

Around him sat his second wife of nine years, Savannah Dare, and their daughter, Sienna, along with their nearest and dearest country club friends. Missing were their other two sons, but they'd show up soon.

Olivia placed a hand on his shoulder. "He loves her, you know. And Mom's made her peace."

"Mom had no choice once she found out about *her*."

Robert Dare had met the much younger Savannah Sheppard and, to hear him tell it, fallen instantly in love. She was now the mother of his three other children, the oldest of whom was twenty-five. Ian had just turned thirty. Anyone could do the math and come up with two families at the same time. The man was beyond fertile, that was for damned sure.

At the reminder, Ian finished his drink and placed the tumbler on a passing server's tray. "I showed my face. I'm out of here." He started for the exit.

"Ian, hold on," his sister said, frustration in her tone.

"What? Do you want me to wait until they sing 'Happy Birthday'? No thanks. I'm leaving."

Before they could continue the discussion, their half brother Alex strode through the double door entrance with a spectacular-looking woman holding tightly to his arm, and Ian's plans changed.

Because of *her*.

Some people had presence; others merely wished they possessed that magic something. In her bold, red dress and fuck-me heels, she owned the room. And he wanted to own her. Petite and curvy with long, chocolate-brown hair that fell down her back in wild curls, she was the antithesis of every too-thin female he'd dated and kept at arm's length. But she was with his half brother, which meant he had to steer clear.

"I thought you were leaving," Olivia said from beside him.

"I am." He should. If he could tear his gaze away from *her*.

"If you wait for Tyler and Scott, you might just relax enough to have fun," she said of their brothers. "Come on, please?" Olivia used the pleading tone he never could resist.

"Yeah, please, Ian? Come on," his sister Avery said, joining them, looking equally mature in a silver gown that showed way too much cleavage. At twenty-two, she was similar in coloring and looks to Olivia, and he wasn't any more ready to think of her as a grown-up—never mind letting other men ogle her—than he was with her sister.

Ian set his jaw, amazed these two hadn't been the death of him yet.

"So what am I begging him to do?" Avery asked Olivia.

Olivia grinned. "I want him to stay and hang out for a while. Having fun is probably out of the question, but I'm trying to persuade him to let loose."

"Brat," he muttered, unable to hold back a smile at Olivia's persistence.

He stole another glance at his lady in red. He could no more leave than he could approach her, he thought, frustrated because he was a man of action, and right now, he could do nothing but watch her.

"Well?" Olivia asked.

He forced his gaze to his sister and smiled. "Because you two asked so nicely, I'll stay." But his attention remained on the woman now dancing and laughing with his half brother.

Riley Taylor felt his eyes on her from the moment she entered the elegantly decorated ballroom on the arm of another man. As it was, her heels made it difficult enough to maneuver gracefully. Knowing a devastatingly sexy man watched her every move only made not falling on her ass even more of a challenge.

Alex Dare, her best friend, was oblivious. Being the star quarterback of the Tampa Breakers meant he was used to stares and attention. Riley wasn't. And since this was his father's birthday bash, he knew everyone here. She didn't.

She definitely didn't know *him*. She'd managed to avoid this annual party in the past with a legitimate work excuse one year, the flu another, but this year, Alex knew she was down in the dumps due to job problems, and he'd insisted she come along and have a good time.

While Alex danced with his mother, then sister, she headed for the bar and asked the bartender for a glass of ice water. She took a sip and turned to go find a seat, someplace where she could get off her feet and slip free of her offending heels.

She'd barely taken half a step when she bumped into a hard, suit-clad body. The accompanying jolt sent her water spilling from the top of her glass and into her cleavage. The chill startled her as much as the liquid that dripped down her chest.

"Oh!" She teetered on her stilettos, and big, warm hands grasped her shoulders, steadying her.

She gathered herself and looked up into the face of the man she'd been covertly watching. "You," she said on a breathy whisper.

His eyes, indigo with a hint of light blue in the depths, sparkled in amusement and something more. "Glad you noticed me too."

She blinked, mortified, no words rushing into her brain to save her. She was too busy taking him in. Dark-brown hair stylishly cut, cheekbones perfectly carved, and a strong jaw completed the package. And the most intense heat emanated from his touch as he held on to her arms. His big hands made her feel small, not an easy feat when she was always conscious of her too-full curves.

She breathed in deeply and was treated to a masculine, woodsy scent that turned her insides to pure mush. Full-scale awareness rocked her to her core. This man hit all her right buttons.

"Are you all right?" he asked.

"I'm fine." Or she would be if he'd release her so she could think. Instead of telling him so, she continued to stare into his handsome face.

"You certainly are," he murmured.

A heated flush rushed to her cheeks at the compliment, and a delicious warmth invaded her system.

"I'm sorry about the spill," he said.

At least she hoped he was oblivious to her ridiculous attraction to him.

"You're wet." He released her and reached for a napkin from the bar.

Yes, she was. In wholly inappropriate ways considering they'd barely met. Desire pulsed through her veins. Oh my God, what was it about this man that caused reactions in her body another man would have to work overtime to achieve?

He pressed the thin paper napkin against her chest and neck. He didn't linger, didn't stroke her anywhere he shouldn't, but she could swear she felt the heat of his fingertips against her skin. Between his heady scent and his deliberate touch, her nerves felt raw and exposed. Her breasts swelled, her nipples peaked, and she shivered, her body tightening in places she'd long thought dormant. If he noticed, he was too much of a gentleman to say.

No man had ever awakened her senses this way before. Sometimes she wondered if that was a deliberate choice on her part. *Obviously not,* she thought and forced herself to step back, away from his potent aura.

He crinkled the napkin and placed the paper onto the bar.

"Thank you," she said.

"My pleasure." The word, laced with sexual innuendo, rolled off his tongue, and his eyes darkened to a deep indigo, an indication that this crazy attraction she experienced wasn't one-sided.

"Maybe now we can move on to introductions. I'm Ian Dare," he said.

She swallowed hard, disappointment rushing through her as she realized, for all her awareness of him, he was the one man at this party she ought to stay away from. "Alex's brother."

"Half brother," he bit out.

"Yes." She understood his pointed correction. Alex wouldn't want any more of a connection to Ian than Ian did to Alex.

"You have your father's eyes," she couldn't help but note.

His expression changed, going from warm to cold in an instant. "I hope that's the only thing you think that bastard and I have in common."

Riley raised her eyebrows at the bitter tone. Okay, she understood he had his reasons, but she was a stranger.

Ian shrugged, his broad shoulders rolling beneath his tailored, dark suit. "What can I say? Only a bastard would live two separate lives with two separate families at the same time."

"You do lay it out there," she murmured.

His eyes glittered like silver ice. "It's not like everyone here doesn't know it."

Though she ought to change the subject, he'd been open, so she decided to ask what was on her mind. "If you're still so angry with him, why come for his birthday?"

"Because my sisters asked me to," he said, his tone turning warm and indulgent.

A hint of an easier expression changed his face from hard and unyielding to devastatingly sexy once more.

"Avery and Olivia are much more forgiving than me," he explained.

She smiled at his obvious affection for his siblings. As an only child, she envied them a caring, older brother. At least she'd had Alex, she thought and glanced around looking for the man who'd brought her here. She found him on the dance floor, still with his mother, and relaxed.

"Back to introductions," Ian said. "You know my name; now it's your turn."

"Riley Taylor."

"Alex's girlfriend," he said with disappointment. "I saw you two walk in."

That's what he thought? "No, we're friends. More like brother and sister than anything else."

His eyes lit up, and she caught a glimpse of yet another expression—pleasantly surprised. "That's the best news I've heard all night," he said in a deep, compelling tone, his hot gaze never leaving hers.

At a loss for words, Riley remained silent.

"So, Ms. Riley Taylor, where were you off to in such a hurry?" he asked.

"I wanted to rest my feet," she admitted.

He glanced down at her legs, taking in her red pumps. "Ahh. Well, I have just the place."

Before she could argue—and if she'd realized he'd planned to drag her off alone, she might have—Ian grasped her arm and guided her to the exit at the far side of the room.

"Ian—"

"Shh. You'll thank me later. I promise." He pushed open the door, and they stepped out onto a deck that wasn't in use this evening.

Sticky night air surrounded them, but being a Floridian, she was used to it, and obviously so was he. His arm still cupping her elbow, he led her to a small love seat and gestured for her to sit.

She sensed he was a man who often got his way, and though she'd never found that trait attractive before, on him, it worked. She settled into the soft cushions. He did the same, leaving no space between them, and she liked the feel of his hard body aligned with hers. Her heart beat hard in her chest, excitement and arousal pounding away inside her.

Around them, it was dark, the only light coming from sconces on the nearby building.

"Put your feet up." He pointed to the table in front of them.

"Bossy," she murmured.

Ian grinned. He was, and damn proud of it. "You're the one who said your feet hurt," he reminded her.

"True." She shot him a sheepish look that was nothing short of adorable.

The reverberation in her throat went straight to Ian's cock, and he shifted in his seat, pure sexual desire now pumping through his veins.

He'd been pissed off and bored at his father's ridiculous birthday gala. Even his sisters had barely been able to coax a smile from him. Then *she'd* walked into the room.

Because she was with his half brother, Ian hadn't planned on approaching her, but the minute he'd caught sight of her alone at the bar, he'd gone after her, compelled by a force beyond his understanding. Finding out she and Alex were just friends had made his night because she'd provide a perfect distraction to the pain that followed him whenever his father's other family was near.

"Shoes?" he reminded her.

She dipped her head and slipped off her heels, moaning in obvious relief.

"That sound makes me think of other things," he said, capturing her gaze.

"Such as?" She unconsciously swayed closer, and he suppressed a grin.

"Sex. With you."

"Oh." Her lips parted with the word, and Ian couldn't tear his gaze away from her lush, red-painted mouth.

A mouth he could envision many uses for, none of them tame.

"Is this how you charm all your women?" she asked. "Because I'm not sure it's working." A teasing smile lifted her lips, contradicting her words.

He had her, all right, as much as she had him.

He kept his gaze on her face, but he wasn't a complete gentleman and couldn't resist brushing his hand over her tight nipples showing through the fabric of her dress.

Her eyes widened in surprise at the same time a soft moan escaped, sealing her fate. He slid one arm across the love seat until his fingers hit her mass of curls, and he wrapped his hand in the thick strands. Then, tugging her close, he sealed his mouth over hers. She opened for him immediately. The first taste was a mere preview, not nearly enough, and he deepened the kiss, taking more.

Sweet, hot, and her tongue tangled with his. He gripped her hair harder, wanting still more. She was like all his favorite vices in one delectable package. Best of all, she kissed him back, every inch a willing, giving partner.

He was a man who dominated and took, but from the minute he tasted her, he gave as well. If his brain were clear, he'd have pulled back immediately, but she reached out and gripped his shoulders, curling her fingers through the fabric of his shirt, her nails digging into his skin. Each thrust of his tongue in her mouth mimicked what he really wanted, and his cock hardened even more.

"You've got to be kidding me," his half brother said, interrupting at the worst possible moment.

He would have taken his time, but Riley jumped, pushing at his chest and backing away from him at the same time.

"Alex!"

"Yeah. The guy who brought you here, remember?"

Ian cursed his half brother's interruption as much as he welcomed the reminder that this woman represented everything Ian resented. His half brother's friend. Alex, with whom he had a rivalry that would have done real siblings proud.

The oldest sibling in the *other* family was everything Ian wasn't. Brash, loud, tattoos on his forearms, and he threw a mean football as quarterback of the Tampa Breakers. Ian, meanwhile, was more of a thinker, president of the Breakers' rivals, the Miami Thunder, owned by his father's estranged brother, Ian's uncle.

Riley jumped up, smoothing her dress and rubbing at her swollen lips, doing nothing to ease the tension emanating from her best friend.

Ian took his time standing.

"I see you met my brother," Alex said, his tone tight.

Riley swallowed hard. "We were just—"

"Getting better acquainted," Ian said in a seductive tone meant to taunt Alex and imply just how much better he now knew Riley.

A muscle ticked in the other man's jaw. "Ready to go back inside?" Alex asked her.

Neither one of them would make a scene at this mockery of a family event.

"Yes." She didn't meet Ian's gaze as she walked around him and came up alongside Alex.

"Good, because my dad's been asking for you. He said it's been too long since he's seen you," Alex said, taunting Ian back with the mention of the one person sure to piss him off.

Despite knowing better, Ian took the bait. "Go on. We were finished anyway," he said, dismissing Riley as surely as she'd done to him.

Never mind that she was obviously torn between her friend and whatever had just happened between them; she'd chosen

Alex. A choice Ian had been through before and come out on the same wrong end.

In what appeared to be a deliberately possessive move, Alex wrapped an arm around her waist and led her back inside. Ian watched, ignoring the twisting pain in his gut at the sight. Which was ridiculous. He didn't have any emotional investment in Riley Taylor. He didn't do emotion, period. He viewed relationships through the lens of his father's adultery, finding it easier to remain on the outside looking in.

Distance was his friend. Sex worked for him. It was love and commitment he distrusted. So no matter how different that brief moment with Riley had been, that was all it was.

A moment.

One that would never happen again.

Riley followed Alex onto the dance floor in silence. They hadn't spoken a word to each other since she'd let him lead her away from Ian. She understood his shocked reaction and wanted to soothe his frazzled nerves but didn't know how. Not when her own nerves were so raw from one simple kiss.

Except nothing about Ian was simple, and that kiss left her reeling. From the minute his lips touched hers, everything else around her had ceased to matter. The tug of arousal hit her in the pit of her stomach, in her scalp as his fingers tugged her hair, in the weight of her breasts, between her thighs and, most telling, in her mind. He was a strong man, the kind who knew what he wanted and who liked to get his way. The type of man she usually avoided and for good reason.

But she'd never experienced chemistry so strong before. His pull was so compelling that she'd willingly followed him outside regardless of the fact that she knew without a doubt her closest friend in the world would be hurt if she got close to Ian.

"Are you going to talk to me?" Alex asked, breaking into her thoughts.

"I'm not sure what to say."

On the one hand, he didn't have a say in her personal life. She didn't owe him an apology. On the other, he was her everything. The child she'd grown up next door to and the best friend who'd saved her sanity and given her a safe haven from her abusive father.

She was wrong. She knew exactly what to say. "I'm sorry."

He touched his forehead to hers. "I don't know what came over me. I found you two kissing, and I saw red."

"It was just chemistry." She let out a shaky laugh, knowing that term was too benign for what had passed between her and Ian.

"I don't want you to get hurt. The man doesn't do relationships, Ri. He uses women and moves on."

"Umm, pot/kettle?" she asked him. Alex moved from woman to woman just as he'd accused his half brother of doing.

He'd even kissed *her* once. Horndog that he was, he said he'd had to try, but they both agreed there was no spark, and their friendship meant way too much to throw away for a quick tumble between the sheets.

Alex frowned. "Maybe so, but that doesn't change the facts about him. I don't want you to get hurt."

"I won't," she assured him, even as her heart picked up speed when she caught sight of Ian watching them from across the room.

Drink in hand, brooding expression on his face, his stare never wavered.

She curled her hands into the suit fabric covering Alex's shoulders and assured herself she was telling the truth.

"What if he was using you to get to me?"

"Because the man can't be interested in me for me?" she asked, her pride wounded despite the fact that Alex was just trying to protect her.

Alex slowed his steps and leaned back to look into her eyes. "That's not what I meant, and you know it. Any man would be lucky to have you, and I'd never get between you and the right guy." A muscle pulsed in Alex's right temple, a sure sign of tension and stress. "But Ian's not that guy."

She swallowed hard, hating that he just might be right. Riley wasn't into one-night stands. Which was why her body's combustible reaction to Ian Dare confused and confounded her. How far would she have let him go if Alex hadn't inter-rupted? Much further than she'd like to imagine, and her body responded with a full-out shiver at the thought.

"Now can we forget about him?"

Not likely, she thought, when his gaze burned hotter than his kiss. Somehow she managed to swallow over the lump in her throat and give Alex the answer he sought. "Sure."

Pleased, Alex pulled her back into his arms to continue their slow dance. Around them, other guests, mostly his father's age, moved slowly in time to the music.

"Did I mention how much I appreciate you coming here with me?" Obviously trying to ease the tension between them, he shot her the same charming grin that had women thinking they were special.

Riley knew better. She *was* special to him, and if he ever turned his brand of protectiveness on the right kind of woman and not the groupies he preferred, he might find himself settled and happy one day. Sadly, he didn't seem to be on that path.

She decided to let their disagreement over Ian go. "I believe you've mentioned how wonderful I am a couple of times. But you still owe me one," Riley said. Parties like this weren't her thing.

"It took your mind off your job stress, right?" he asked.

She nodded. "Yes, and let's not even talk about that right now." Monday was soon enough to deal with her new boss.

"You got it. Ready for a break?" he asked.

She nodded. Unable to help herself, she glanced over where she'd seen Ian earlier, but he was gone. The

disappointment twisting the pit of her stomach was dispro-
portional to the amount of time she'd known him, and she
blamed that kiss.

Her lips still tingled, and if she closed her eyes and ran
her tongue over them, she could taste his heady, masculine
flavor. Somehow she had to shake him from her thoughts.
Alex's reaction to seeing them together meant Riley
couldn't allow herself the luxury of indulging in anything
more with Ian.

Not even in her thoughts or dreams.

Get *Dare to Love* now at your
local bookstore or buy online!

ABOUT THE AUTHOR

Carly Phillips is the *New York Times* and *USA Today* bestselling author of more than fifty sexy contemporary romance novels featuring hot men, strong women, and the emotionally compelling stories her readers have come to expect and love. Carly's career spans over a decade and a half with various New York publishing houses, and she is now an indie author who runs her own business and loves every exciting minute of her publishing journey. Carly is  happily married to her college sweetheart and is the mother of two nearly adult daughters and three crazy dogs (two wheaten terriers and one mutant Havanese) who star on her Facebook fan page and website. Carly loves social media and is always around to interact with her readers. You can find out more about Carly at www.carlyphillips.com.

Carly's Booklist by Series

Dare to Love Series

Book 1: *Dare to Love* (Ian & Riley)
Book 2: *Dare to Desire*
(Alex & Madison)
Book 3: *Dare to Touch*
(Olivia & Dylan)
Book 4: *Dare to Hold* (Scott & Meg)
Book 5: *Dare to Rock* (Avery & Grey)
Book 6: *Dare to Take* (Tyler & Ella)

NY Dares Series

Book 1: *Dare to Surrender*
(Gabe & Isabelle)
Book 2: *Dare to Submit*
(Decklan & Amanda)
Book 3: *Dare to Seduce*
(Max & Lucy)

*The NY Dares books are
more erotic/hotter books.

Serendipity Series

Serendipity
Destiny
Karma

Serendipity's Finest Series

Perfect Fit
Perfect Fling
Perfect Together

Serendipity Novellas

Fated
Hot Summer Nights
(Perfect Stranger)

Bachelor Blog Series

Kiss Me If You Can
Love Me If You Dare

Lucky Series

Lucky Charm
Lucky Streak
Lucky Break

Ty and Hunter Series

Cross My Heart
Sealed with a Kiss

Hot Zone Series

Hot Stuff
Hot Number
Hot Item
Hot Property

Costas Sisters Series

Summer Lovin'
Under the Boardwalk

Chandler Brothers Series

The Bachelor
The Playboy
The Heartbreaker

Stand-Alone Titles

Brazen
Seduce Me
Secret Fantasy
The Right Choice
Suddenly Love
Perfect Partners
Unexpected Chances
Worthy of Love

Keep up with Carly and her upcoming books:

Website:
www.carlyphillips.com

Sign up for blog and website updates:
www.carlyphillips.com/category/blog/

Sign up for Carly's newsletter:
www.carlyphillips.com/newsletter-sign-up

Carly on Facebook:
www.facebook.com/CarlyPhillipsFanPage

Carly on Twitter:
www.twitter.com/carlyphillips

Hang out at Carly's Corner—hot guys & giveaways!
smarturl.it/CarlysCornerFB